THE
POWER
FICTION OF

THE
POWER
FICTION OF

GEM SCORP / KUYA JAP

Library of Congress Control Number: 2012901156
ISBN: Hardcover   978-1-4691-5522-7
                 Softcover   978-1-4691-5521-0
                 Ebook   978-1-4691-5523-4

To order additional copies of this book, contact:
Xlibris Corporation
1-888-795-4274
www.Xlibris.com
Orders@Xlibris.com
111128

Contents

Dear Reader,

The Power of Fiction is my collection of fictional stories in which I try to develop different characters of myself in various situations. The stories reflect my personal background, culture, fantasies, and principles in life and how I deal with my daily encounter with dilemmas. Although most of the stories here are centered on love and romance, this book will also tell you what made Filipinos survive better than any other race in the world when it comes to struggles with life.

I sincerely hope you enjoy reading my first fictional book as much as I enjoyed writing it.

With warm regards and thanks,
Gem Scorp

Acknowledgements

I would like to say my special thank you to "**Mengkay**," a woman whose emotion is stronger than anyone else that I've ever known. Her love is a typical Filipina way of loving who is willing to give up everything just for the sake of love and to be loved. A woman who knows no pain or suffering just to be with the one she dearly loves. I thank you for the love you bestowed on me—a love I could never repay.

To my dearest "**Iyaan**" whom I kept my love hidden for over 15 years and whose story proved that love can survive over the test of time. Because of "**Iyaan**" I started to dream, to dream of big things and most of these dreams are now coming into a reality.

I'd like to express my sincerest thanks to my "**Bunso**" who helped me bring out the words for the creation of most of the stories in this book. I thank her for the great inspiration she gave me. Her presence was adrenaline to my creative thinking.

I would like to take this opportunity to thank my dearest friend in New York who started as my patient. Our common interest in writing poetry brought as closer together. I'm happy and proud to introduce my dear friend **Ms. Carol Gossman** who edits not only my paper work but also some areas of my life.

In my thirty years of existence, I met two great friends who knew most of my "being" and who supported me without doubts. They are the ones who cried and cheered me up and made me drunk at times just to see the brighter side of the world. I call them my "angels" and my "demons" **Ms. Jacqueline Suelto—Tan** and **Ms. Kenneth joy Sta. Maria**. I thank you ladies because we became a great team.

I would never forget to pay special respect to my best friend of all friends—**Ms. Jenette Sardan-Bantug**. Since the time I met her, our hearts and thoughts were intertwined together. Our closeness made other jealous yet we remained best of friends.

Finally, I would like to say thank you to ***the woman I dearly love now***—the one who took the sadness out of me. After years of being sad and alone, after suffering from the curse of being unloved and rejected, she made me believe that life is beautiful. And indeed life is beautiful because I found beauty in her sight. The love I found in her made me chase for her love twice and I'm willing to remarry her every time she will say "I do." I call her my "**P**rincess."

Princess, "I always say I love you not because I love to repeat it, but because it is the most truthful feeling I know, and I don't know how to say it better."

Gem Scorp

Liberato

Cold tears flowed steadily from Liberato's weary eyes as he sipped his coffee. He was sitting on a wooden chair beside his father's bed in one of the isolation rooms of the Provincial Hospital. The dingy walls seemed to close in on him the longer he sat watching his father. The old man lay on the bed, slowly wasting away because of his illness.

Liberato knew that he should feel distraught. His father, after all, was dying. But he was numb. The numbness alternated with feelings of hatred rather than pity and anguish instead of hope, feelings brought on by years of clamoring for his father's love and attention, which the old man was never able to give. Suddenly, a gush of bright red blood spurted from his father's mouth and nose. Liberato jumped up and grabbed the syringe that lay on the tray beside his father, as well as the clear vial of emergency drug meant to stop his father from bleeding. But before he could act, his father grabbed his hand and said in a low, horse voice, "Son, do you love me? Truly love me?" The old man's tired, teary eyes looked up to him, and Liberato could feel his heart breaking. He tried to open his mouth to answer, but couldn't. A lump the size of a baseball was lodged in his throat. He let go from his father's hold and took a piece of rag to wipe away the blood that started to dry up on the floor as he hastily wiped the tears that welled up in his eyes. As he wiped away the dirty blood, memories of his childhood flashed before his eyes. One incident stood out in particular.

"No me amor my son." He had overhead his father blurt these words while sitting with his drinking buddies one summer afternoon. "He is gay." He and his friends laughed, the other men giving him sympathetic pats on the back.

My father thinks I'm gay? He remembered asking himself.

Recollections of this incident would send angry surges of emotion through his veins like a racing V8 engine in a Corvette. Painful memories of how he was bullied as a child and how his father embarrassed him in front of his drinking buddies would haunt him even when he became an adult. In school he faced the cruel taunts of classmates who picked at his sliced ears. His ears were deformed, separated into three parts that made it look like someone had taken a machete and sliced his ears out of spite.

Playmates loved to tease him about the four stubs that substituted for fingers on his deformed left hand. Older kids mimicked him mercilessly when he stuttered. Because of the humiliation, Liberato decided to isolate himself, to shy away from other people in order to avoid the endless jokes. But he was not gay.

He was not bothered by being called a "gay." What hurt him was finding out that the word "amor" means "love." It hurt him badly finding out his father didn't love him at all. Knowing that his father was not shy about telling the world of this sentiment made the cut deeper.

"Ga! (darling). "Ga! (darling). His girlfriend had entered the room. She knelt down and helped him wipe the blood from the floor.

"I'm sorry," Liberato apologized.

"That's okay," she said.

His girlfriend noticed the redness of his eyes and realized that he had been crying. "Go sit," she said softly, giving him a soft peck on the cheek. 'I'll take care of this."

How is your father?" she asked as she brushed the floor.

Liberato was silent.

"I never asked my father to bring me to this world," he said. "He is responsible for my being here and for all these birth defects!" he continued bitterly. "So he is obligated to act as my father and to love me as his son. But he never did. And I did not mind asking for his love. Seeing him show no love for me, and giving my brother all the love he could muster killed me every time."

"That's not true," his girlfriend said. "He loved you. He was just not good at showing it, that's all."

Liberato shook his head angrily. "It is!"

His lips were shaking and his face turned red as he stood up and smashed his closed fist against the wall, sending a small shower of plaster falling down next to his father's bed. His teeth made grinding sounds as every word escaped from his mouth. He had graduated from elementary school with honors and was very excited to tell his parents. He was also excited to know what gift they had prepared for him for that special day. However, upon reaching home, his father broke the news. There was no gift. They had bought something expensive for his little brother, and no money was left for a gift for him.

"Nothing for a second placer," he mumbled. "That was how they thought of me. I did not deserve anything from them."

He continued telling the story. He was able to save his lunch money by not eating during school recess for two months. At the end of the second month he was able to buy a gift for himself, a cheap video game that he got by haggling with the old man at the local toy store. He wanted his parents to give the video game to him as a gift when that day came for him to receive his award. He anticipated the arrival of graduation day, imagining the look on everyone's face when they would see him receiving his gift from his parents. However, only his mother was there when graduation day came. She came up the narrow cement stairs that led to the stage. When Liberato realized that his father was not following closely behind, he tried to freeze his smile as best as he could. If he didn't, tears would have started falling down his small cheeks and into the crisp, starched white shirt that his mother had carefully ironed for him the night before. His mother gave him his gift, the video game that he had bought with the money he had saved, and gave him a small kiss on the check after pinning the small red ribbon of merit on his shirt.

"I was a hopeless child," he sobbed.

"My father did not love me for he thought I was a gay. And I never got first honors in school like my little brother did. And with all these birth defects, how could he ever love me? I'm a waste for him," he said angrily. "Not worthy enough to love."

However, he was able to prove everybody wrong, specially his father. Despite his condition he was able to land a high-paying job in the city. In some strange way, his handicap paved the way for the little bit of success in his life. His defects fueled his drive to be good at work, and it was able to help him get his family out of the clutches of poverty.

The same poverty that made Liberato an unwanted child, his grandmother told him once. His parents tried to have him aborted when they learned that his mother was pregnant. They were both young and were unmarried. To make matters worse, his father's family did not approve of his mother—too poor to be married to his father. However, they could not do the abortion. The two decided to elope, and because of this his father lost his inheritance. Despite the attempted abortion Liberato survived, but not unscathed. His deformities silently told the story of how unwanted he was by his own parents.

Liberato took out his wallet, which was stuffed full of bills—medical bills, receipts for medications, doctor's fees. He realized how much he had spent for his father's hospitalization. "I could have used this money for our wedding, he said, "looking at his girlfriend." Instead, I'm squandering all this money on the man who never spent a penny on me."

As he looked at the bills he remembered how his father worked hard just to provide one full meal a day for his family. His father would stay up all night making candies to sell in the morning. He would walk miles the next day just to reach his customers. Afterward, his father would hitch a ride on a bus and head for the city, where he had a job shining shoes on the corner of a small barbershop. During the evenings he earned small pennies by fetching water for the neighbors before sitting down on his small, rickety stool after dinner to continue making candies. "When you got a family, you'll do everything for them because you love them," his mother used to tell him. But Liberato was not satisfied. He never understood, not as a kid, and not even when he became an adult. His brother always got something out of his father's toil—a shiny new plastic truck, a brand new yo-yo that flashed with different colors as it slid up and down. Every time a new toy came, the older ones would be passed on to him. He was getting his younger brother's hand-me-downs. He learned to play with other toys, toys he made himself. He would tell himself each time that he was capable of getting toys for himself without having to ask his father. But deep down, he was hurt and resented his brother's shouts of glee every time a new toy came.

"He never loved me, Mom," he would yell at his mother during heated arguments. "He only cared about my brother, but never for me!"

"Son, your father only knew construction work before," his mother would answer sadly, not knowing what else to say.

Too much hard work, too little sleep took a toll on his father's health. He got sicker and sicker, and soon enough he became too sick to hold down his three jobs. Tuberculosis turned his shoulders inwards, giving him the look of a stooped, old man. He grew thinner and thinner because he had lost his appetite. Neighbors started avoiding them, fearful that they would get the disease from his father or from any other member of the family. Even though Liberato was no longer living at home, he could feel the stares, the whispered gossip as he passed the houses of the neighbors every time he came home.

However, despite all the resentment that he had for his father, he was also fearful. His father was dying. This could be his last moments with the man. Liberato was at a loss as to what to do. He was angry and wanted nothing to do with his father. Yet, this man, the only father he ever knew, lay dying.

"If you love me, you must help your brother finish his studies and find him a job before you get married to any woman." This was what his father told him right after he landed a job in the city. And he wanted his father to love him. So he agreed. But now, he wanted to be free of his promise. He was torn between wanting to grant his father's dying wishes and not caring about his father for once.

"'Tang (dad), I have always obeyed you and I wanted to please you because I love you so much," Liberato quietly whispered as he looked at the frail figure of his father.

His father was already awake, quietly gasping for breath as he gazed at his son. Liberato continued, "I tried my best to please you, but nothing I did could ever make you love me. All you could see was my brother." A strong glint of protest passed over his father's eyes after Liberato said the words. His father tried to shake his head as vigorously as he could. He had given up on trying to speak. He was hoarse and all he could give out were short, hoarse grunts that exhausted his weak frame.

"I have my own life now, Tang," Liberato added. Despite his desire to lash out at his father, Liberato could not help but be gentle to the old man, now looking up at him with sad, teary eyes. What did he see in those eyes? Regret? Pity? Fear? Liberato didn't know, and his desire to tell his father all that he wanted to say for almost thirty years made it easier not to find out.

He wanted to be free of his promise. He wanted to stop shouldering the responsibility of looking after his brother, who did not seem interested in finishing his studies. Carlo landed in a drug rehab center after Liberato found packets of marijuana in his room. His father knew nothing about this. All they knew was that Carlo was almost ready to finish the engineering course that his father and mother wanted him to take. His parents were proud of Carlo, even though Carlo was rarely home.

BEEP! BEEP! BEEP! The respirator and ventilator attached to his father went off simultaneously, jolting Liberato from his reverie. Surprisingly, his father lay peaceful on the bed. It took him a minute to realize that his father was no longer breathing. Liberato pulled the call bell for help, sprang towards the door and stuck his head out.

"Nurse, help!" he shouted at the top of his lungs. The nurses and the attendant rushed to the room, and Liberato stood near the door, sobbing, not knowing what to do. He looked around for his girlfriend but she was gone. She had gone home after cleaning up the blood to get some rest. Liberato wished that his mother, even his brother, was there. "Not like this," he muttered shakily as he stood watching the nurse work on his father. "Not like this."

Moments later, the doctor declared Gaspar Aquino dead. Liberato was no longer numb. Had he said all that he wanted to say? He desperately wanted his father alive, ready to listen to him. There was still so much left unsaid, and so many things that he desperately wanted to hear from his father.

It was now a few hours after his father had been declared dead. Liberato was sitting in the waiting area, holding his father's meager belongings—a piece of spare T-shirt and the bloody rags they used to wipe his lips—while waiting for the death certificate to be given out.

"Sir, I think this is for you," the young guy said.

"What is this?" he asked.

"I found this under your father's bed."

Liberato looked at the envelope in his hand. It was crumpled, with browned edges, as if someone has been holding it for a long time. He opened the envelope and found that it contained a letter from his father. One whole page of his father's scrawny, shaky handwriting was in front of him. For a moment, Liberato remembered that his father never finished high school and that writing was difficult for him.

And yet, he wrote me a letter, he thought, surprised.

In the letter, his father apologized for everything from attempting to abort his mother's pregnancy, to being emotionally distant while he was growing up.

My son, my first son, I wanted you and I always wanted to have a son," his father told him in the letter. *"I was young, and I was afraid of my parents. This is perhaps the biggest reason why we decided for an abortion. However, when we failed, I took that as a sign. You were meant for us and that is why I became excited to have you. I chose to suffer losing my inheritance because I wanted you so much.*

I wanted you to learn how to survive rather than be dependent on anybody; thus, I tried to make you see that I love your brother more than you," his father added. *"I knew that the world will be cruel to you, with your appearance and your handicap. I wanted to make you strong, even if it meant having you hate me for being so cruel.*

I love you, my son. Please forgive me.

The letter ended with his father giving him the rights to their home and all their land. He also revealed that he knew of his girlfriend and his plans to marry.

I have known for a long time. I am glad that you have found a woman who loves you for who you are. My only wish is that you name your first child after me.

Liberato closed the letter, tears cascading down his eyes. "Forgive me, father for ever doubting your love."

Strange

"God, gimme someone whom I could be comfortable with. Someone who could take good care of my two kids," Chevy whispered in a heartfelt prayer when she stepped out of her office. She then walked across the street to where her car was parked.

"Miss, can I carry your bags?" a stranger volunteered. The man was in his 30s. He was wearing a red hat with its tip facing backward, an oversized shirt, and a pair of jeans that was hanging below his waist line.

Who is this stranger? Chevy wondering. I don't talk to this type of person living in the street. Chevy couldn't decide but . . .

"Thank you, mister. You may carry them."

"Hey. Hey. Hey. I didn't mean it." The man was apologetic.

"What? You asked me if you could carry my bags and you didn't mean it?"

"I dunno. I never talk to decent people like you, especially a pretty, sexy girl like you."

Chevy drew a smile.

Right after the prayer, a stranger had come to her who didn't know what he was saying and why he talking to decent people he normally didn't talk to. Coincidence or God's freaking answer?

"You know what, just pick up my bags and come with me to my house," Chevy requested. "I'm Chevy."

"Mustang."

Both spent their time together inside Chevy's Honda coupe. Chevy learned that Mustang was a Jamaican guy who was jobless; with no family, and without education.

"Oh wow," Mustang yelled. "Your house?" he asked as his fingers were pointed to a big house well situated in a very costly subdivision of Long Island City, New York.

"Yes. Come on in." She parked in her underground garage.

As an interior designer, Chevy was able to improve her house and her Spanish heritage style radiated from every corner of the house. Her very spacious home could accommodate a show like Oprah's. The Asian type landscape of her lawn glamorized the exotic terrain of the subdivision.

"My kids," Chevy said, introducing Mustang to her kids.

Chevy noted Mustang's interest in kids. Her kids welcomed Mustang as if they knew him very well. Chevy cried some tears as she recalled her prayers. Be really careful what you asked for, Chevy reminded herself.

"I could take care of your kids," Mustang said, breaking Chevy's silence.

"What? Are you serious?"

"Yes. And you could save money."

Chevy accepted the offer. She couldn't believe she trusted this stranger whom she just met this morning.

"I'll come back tomorrow morning and start my new job, right?" Mustang asked.

Chevy's smart brain didn't work but she nodded as if she fully understood what was going on.

The days passed fast and Chevy found herself on the bed reminiscing about the events of the days, when thoughts of her boyfriend came to her mind and were bothering her.

"Will you marry me?" Chevy's boyfriend's proposal was just said in a very untimely manner and Chevy had no answer at that time. Her relationship with her boyfriend was fine but something was missing. She was not comfortable with him. He bought her expensive perfumes, dresses, and luxury cars. But these things made her feel awkward with her boyfriend. He is too professional and doesn't like kids, Chevy reminded herself. After Chevy refused her boyfriend's proposal, their relationship was cold and she didn't hear anything from him. Finally she went back to sleep but her mind was filled with questions and doubts.

It was 8 in the morning when Chevy was awakened by a noise from the kitchen. She grabbed her pajamas, loaded her gun and headed where the noise was coming from. To her surprise, her kids were sitting at the table having breakfast, they were already dressed for school and she found Mustang was still busy with cooking.

"I'm preparing your breakfast," Mustang said to Chevy.

Chevy moved to him and whispered, "Next time, call me first or otherwise you will see yourself in the morgue."

The breakfast was good; Chevy learned that Mustang could cook. And Mustang dropped the kids off at their school. From Monday to Friday, Mustang did the same routine: cooking and babysitting the kids. Chevy realized how good the relationship between the kids and Mustang was, making her happier and more comfortable with Mustang.

"How am I doing, Chevy?" Mustang asked.

"I'm glad for your patience."

"Since tomorrow is Saturday, could I come to do your laundry?"

"You know how to do it?

"I could try."

On Saturday, Chevy was free from work so she babysat the kids. Mustang came and picked-up the laundry and almost 4 hours afterwards he came back with the laundry and handed it to Chevy.

"Mustang!" Chevy's voiced pinched Mustang's ears.

"What?"

Chevy grinned as she saw that her white clothes had turned into polka dots. She thought Mustang knew something about laundry, but it was Mustang's first try.

"Did your mother teach you about laundry?" Chevy's voice made her lungs collapse but still Chevy was happy with Mustang. His determination to learn would show Chevy that he could be a good companion—that there was also something good in him despite his indecent background.

"Just take care of the kids and never touch any laundry again," Chevy said.

Chevy felt sorry for Mustang. He sacrificed a lot of his time just to come early and take care of her kids. Finally, she asked Mustang to stay at her house so that he wouldn't have to travel anymore and he was glad about it.

It was Monday morning when Chevy saw Mustang had washed her car. Everyday, Mustang made her feel great and surprised her with little things.

"May I drive you to your job today?" Mustang volunteered.

"Do you drive?"

"Back home, yes."

After dropping off the kids, Chevy was in her Honda coupe with Mustang then something went wrong.

When they made a "U" turn, Mustang crashed the car into a meter poll at a corner. Chevy was hurt. Her nose was bleeding but she was fine. When Chevy looked for Mustang, she found him running faster than a train and he vanished quickly like a feather through thick smoke. Police officers came and brought Chevy to a nearby hospital. She was angry and disappointed because of Mustang's unexpected reaction to the event.

Chevy didn't hear from Mustang for days. She was angry at him but was worried at the same time.

KRING. KRING. KRING. Chevy's phone rang. An unidentified caller was trying to reach her.

"Hello."

"Are you okay?"

"Mustang?"

"Yes."

Chevy felt a bee bite in her ears but Mustang was apologetic and asked her not to hang up until she could hear what he wanted to say.

"What for? Why should I listen to you? You ran from that accident like a true coward!" She was shaking but she didn't care. "You damn idiot!"

Chevy was about to hang up the phone but she allowed Mustang to say some somehting.

"My papers expired."

Chevy found out that Mustang was an illegal alien for 6 months now, thus he ran after the incident to avoid the police.

"How could you leave me?"

"I'm sorry but I made sure you were okay, and I was sure you were fine."

Chevy felt relief after hearing Mustang's excuse. When he begged to come back, Chevy asked him for few things. She asked him to look for any legal job and to endorse his income to her regardless of the amount. Mustang grabbed the opportunity.

"By the way, where are you now?" Chevy asked.

"New Jersey."

"Oh lord, you ran that far."

Few days later, Chevy heard some commotion from her kitchen. "That must be Mustang now," she said. Her excitement to see Mustang brought her to the kitchen in few strides. She had missed him a lot and wanted to kiss and hug him, but she held back her last move. Did I just miss him? She was doubtful. She pretended not to notice him and just by—passed him and went straight to the fridge.

"I am welcome in this house now?" Chevy saw the sincerity in Mustang's eyes as he gave her an envelope.

"What's this?'

"Open it please."

"$30.00?"

Chevy was so pleased knowing Mustang obeyed her. Does he love me? She was hopeful. The money was Mustang's first salary and not a big amount but was good enough to show that he was sincere and he cared for her.

"Immigration! You work for the immigration?" Chevy's voice couldn't mask the incredulity that she felt about what she had learned after opening the envelope, which contained the seal of his employer at the inner portion of the envelope. She couldn't believe that Mustang, an illegal alien, was working for the immigration department. Mustang coolly explained that it was the agency who fixed his papers.

Days together with Mustang made Chevy feel more comfortable with him. A different feeling she was trying to avoid. Mustang was not telling her anything but there were some gestures that would suggest to her that he liked her. She didn't want to expect more than that.

February was fast approaching and Chevy felt worried. She was used to being with her boyfriend every February 14 but now she hadn't heard anything from her boyfriend yet. Would Mustang take me to dinner? She was wistful. She knew he wanted her for a friend only. Only?

KRING. KRING. KRING. Chevy's phone rang. "An anonymous caller again?" she fumed. A text message she received: Please meet me at 143-5254 2nd avenue by 6:40 this evening. Chevy held her breath because she knew the hotel. The hotel was her fantasy place if ever someone would want to propose to her. Was this a joke? She was excited but angry. "Is the person my boyfriend or Mustang?" she asked. She was positive that her boyfriend had no idea of the place since she had told only Mustang of it and she knew Mustang could never afford it.

Though hesitant, she went to the place to find out who had invited her. The place was situated at the heart of 2nd avenue where tall buildings boast their beauty to the world. And the falling snow made the surrounding so white. The entrance of the hotel looked elegant. She was thinking she was riding a chariot pulled by white horses on her arrival at the place and a red carpet was before her. As she entered, her eyes saw the floral arrangement of gardenia and hydrangea on both sides of the dance hall while pink petals of carnation were scattered evenly on the floor. She took a step towards the reception area. As she walked, she felt the breeze from a water fountain in the middle of the hall. It had different light bulbs that changed color when the serenade from a violin changed each note. Chevy felt she was flying on air. Her heart was happy as she heard her favorite wedding song played with a Palendag. She looked toward where the sound was coming from and was expecting to see no one but Mustang. But to her surprise she found her boyfriend standing next to a wedding cake that was as tall as him. "A wedding cake?" Chevy shouted in her mind. What is he planning? she couldn't stop asking herself.

Four ladies appeared from the corner and they invited Chevy to a dressing room. Chevy was enjoying a full make—over and she was dressed with an ivory bridal gown that had intricate hand-sewn floral embroidery with seed pearls over English netting. The back of the gown was highlighted by three diagonal straps across it. Chevy's fantasy was near completion. She couldn't stop her tears and she promised herself that whoever was responsible of these things, she'd definitely say "yes" if being asked. Chevy eyed herself from a mirror and she saw a princess ready for a groom. "And who's the groom to be?"

There was turbulence outside the dressing room. Chevy went to look and she saw that the water fountain broke and an oval shape wooden stage had emerged from the bottom of the fountain. And there were two bridges, one was connected from the dressing room and the other one was connected to where her boyfriend stood. The stage had disappeared, replaced by a white mantle where a ring lay on top of a book.

Chevy was summoned by her boyfriend to walk towards the stage and she nodded. As she walked, the other two ladies escorted her and covered her eyes for a purpose. And this was for? Chevy just heard, "A surprise." More surprises? Chevy couldn't think of any more surprises. She was thinking of the finale, with her boyfriend asking her with the magical words. Chevy felt the thrill in her heart. Finally her boyfriend would ask her the thing she'd been waiting for and which she had refused at first. But what about Mustang? Chevy knew she was more comfortable with Mustang but where was he now?

Chevy was now at the center stage. She was waiting for her boyfriend to come, but she was hearing footsteps becoming fainter and fainter until she heard the door slam. Then she heard a screeching noise from a car moving away. "Is he leaving me?" Chevy asked herself and she was tempted to remove the cover of eyes but the ladies beside her stopped her. Then she heard the door slam again and more footsteps coming inside. Thank God he's coming back. And now the footsteps stopped beside her and the ladies left them. Someone took her hand. The caress was familiar but she was reluctant to think of anybody now but her boyfriend. Then . . . .

"Will you take my love to be yours for forever?"

Chevy removed the cover from eyes quickly. "Mustang?"

That was the surprise her boyfriend was telling her. "But how did it happen?"

"Do you prefer to know the answers to your question or would you wish to answer my question first?" Mustang offered a lovely smile.

"Yes. Yes. Yes!" Chevy shouted her answer and embraced Mustang endlessly, tears flowing down her cheeks. Finally Mustang took the ring and placed it on her finger. One kiss, and then a series of kisses followed thereafter. The music was playing joyfully and Chevy's fantasy came to reality and her prayers were answers.

"I do."

"I do."

The Ache of My Heart

Mian, a very high profile woman, loving and caring, yet possessive, is driving with her motorbike at Perdices Street of Dumaguete. The traffic light turns yellow and she made a turn to Santa Rosa Street then her phone beeps. "It's them again!" Mian shouted into the phone at the peak of her voice. She couldn't control her strong emotions. She drove her motorcycle speedily without directions and mumbled with harsh words, "Now he's claiming they are not in any special relationship even if they're together most of the time? He's going home late and sometimes not and he's not letting me know where he's at. Every time his phone beeps, he steps away from me, and the neighborhood is talking about them." The traffic light turns yellow again in Colon Street and Mian slows down then she heard a call from someone from a corner.

"Hey Erra, where you heading?" Ricca, her best friend, asked. "Can I go with you?" Ricca insisting.

Mian stops. She does not want to come with Ricca because she's having a terrible moment, yet she does not want Ricca to feel bad at her. She takes Ricca at her backseat then Ricca suggested that they should go to the boulevard near the city's pier to have some fish ball.

"You look so fierce," Ricca said.

"I don't know how to straighten it," Mian replied with tight fist.

While sitting next to each other waiting for their orders of fish ball and soda, Mian started to talk about her boyfriend. She saw her boyfriend and his claimed close-friend, Jen, early this morning. They were riding together on his motorbike. Jen was at the back while her head was leaning to his boyfriend's shoulder.

"Everything changed," Mian affirmed strongly. "He used to pick me up from my office but now he's making a lot of excuses. He takes more care of himself than before: he shaves everyday, uses different cologne, and wears only new clothes and he's at the mirror frequently. He is more conscious of his looks than his younger, teenager brother. What do you think about all these, Ricca?" she asks calmly with teary eyes and shaking lips.

Ricca is silent, shakes her shoulders, and offers fish ball.

Meanwhile Jay is visiting her best friend, Jen.

Jay, a very talented and charming guy, started a conversation with Jen. "I really love sitting on this seawall," he said. "That's why I always want to be here especially before sunset. This place is peaceful and offers me freedom."

Jen said nothing and simply leaned her head on his shoulder. "How can I tell Mian that after three years of living together my feelings don't go beyond than a special friend?" He shook his head in discontentment.

"But if you did not find Naayi, would you feel the same?" Jen seriously asked.

"I can't answer that but I'm glad Naayi woke me up to this reality," he concluded.

"Is it because she dance so well, she has talent in singing, writing, and painting, and she fills your ideal woman, while on the other hand, Mian simply offers her love and company so you found Naayi more lovable than Mian?" Jen asked.

"It's been two years that I've been thinking this over, I must be sure by now," Jay decided.

Jen paused and gazed into Jay's eyes and said, "but wait." Jen holds his hand when he's about to stand and leave. "And your parents?" she asks curiously. "They favor Mian so much and they want nobody else but her, right?"

"huh," Jay said hopelessly. "I tried breaking-up with Mian before and she nearly killed herself if I wasn't there."

"Oh my God," Jen said, surprised.

"The worst thing is," he sobbed "Naayi is getting married in two-weeks time."

"But you can stop Naayi if your parents will negotiate with her parents. And if her parents favor you, then you will be married on the appointed date of her wedding. That's what I know from her tradition, right?"

"I know but my parents prefer Mian," he answered with tears.

"Naayi loves you," Jen whispered, teasing him.

After hearing it, they teased each other and ran after each other like playful kids.

It was four more days before the wedding day. The phone rang. "Jen, come quickly," Jay said to Jen.

At the seawall, Jay and Jen talked sincerely. "All we need to do is to hire people to act as my parents to save Naayi," Jay insisted. Jen thought it a good idea and they began to plan.

Later Jay went to his dad's office. Jay's dad is a highly respected businessman in their city who owns several businesses like a detective agency, human resource for a stage play, and also a director for a commercial television show. "Dad, I know you can handle this business." "If the price is right," his dad said.

Jay started telling his story as his friend's story.

"Wow," his dad said in amazement. "Is the story for real? Does the guy really want Naayi?" And who's this friend of yours?"

"It's me, Dad. It's me." His dad stared at the wall as if no one was around.

"Do you know how many lovebirds we have?" his dad said with a soft and low voice. "Yes it's only three." His dad continued. He told Jay that he'd taken care of their lovebirds for seven years but the parent-lovebirds just gave them a new baby only after his dad gave a new partner to the male lovebird. "My son, you're my only one. I will save Naayi for you but promise me to save Mian for us," his dad begged Jay.

At night Jay waited for Mian in the living room patiently. To his surprise, Mian hugged him from the back and said, "Jen is here this morning,"

Jay couldn't find words to say.

"I had my 38-caliber to her head but she pleaded that before I shot her, she was going to show me a place," Mian said.

Jay remained nailed in silence. "She brought me to the seawall and told me of everything," she continued with eagerness. "After hearing all the stories, I couldn't stop myself from feeling shame and almost shot myself yet Jen assured me that, if I do it, she was going to claim my death to the police officer and be willing to suffer a life sentence for my satisfaction." Mian sat beside him. "I had all of you suffered for my selfishness, for my own happiness," Mian said, starting to weep.

"No, it's not you Mian, it's me," he insisted. "If only I had control of my feelings, I would direct it all in you. I'm so unlucky in losing you." He too wept. "I hate my feelings in resisting your love," he added.

"Can you give your love to me tonight for the first and last time?" Mian pleaded.

"And tomorrow we all will be free," she promised and smiled.

The living room where they are now is so inviting. The bright rays of the moon make some silhouette shadows over the glass window. Jay checked the outside and nobody was there. "Everybody is asleep," Jay whispered in his mind. He lighted two scented candles and the aroma starts to spread in the room.

Jay scanned Mian's body and his eyes stocked at Mian's thinly-layered white mini-skirt. Racing pulses surged from Jay's chest down to his arms and in between his legs. He requested Mian to slightly spread her legs as she stand still. Mian couldn't hold much of the anticipation, she quickly responded to his request and gently thrust her tongue to make Jay wake in desire. Jay felt the muscles in between his legs grew in tense. He swiftly moved next to Mian. Standing next to each other, Jay thrust his tongue and scratched Mian's tongue inch-to-inch. Jay heard the panicky heartbeats of Mian as she softly says *oh ohh ohhh* in chorus. "Touch me more, Jay." Jay pulled Mian's head and bore it under his chest. The excitement of Mian had her tongue made circles around Jay's hard chest and her fingers curled around Jay's flat belly. Jay responded by showering kisses wherever he could reach and suck every sweat that would drop from Mian's body. His bestial desires had his right hand made some circles over the swell of her breast while his left hand danced all over her spine. His touch made Mian's wandered aimlessly. Mian wanted to feel the tightness of his muscles in between his legs that she turned over and leaned towards the wall but keeping her legs slight spread. Jay grabbed her both hands and anchored them to the wall and his tongue roamed from her neck down to the firmed muscle of her back. Mian rewarded his romantic passion by arching her back some more lifting her mini-skirt inch-to-inch. Jay's eyes were riveted and marveled to the fair skin spilling under Mian's mini-skirt and his heart beats raced in pace. He slid his fingers under Mian's top shirt and pulled them up making Mian a perfect nude sketch subject on a canvass. Feeling the aches of his body, Jay satiate his desire by unleashing the front clasp of her bra. The feeling of being half naked made Mian satisfy her hunger of being wanted. Jay continued to give sensual touch over Mian's spine till his fingers met the only-button of Mian's mini-skirt. Feeling frenzied, he clasped the button and dropping the mini-skirt freely to the ground. Mian is now left with a single barrier, her white underwear. Jay's tensed muscle rise in bulk. Excited to feel his taut muscles, Mian reached Jay's thighs and tugged them to her back. "Make me happy now," Mian complained over her soft moans. "I want to touch you more Mian." He skimmed her body from her navel down to her thighs and made circles over her thighs till he reached the silky lining of her panty. Mian felt panicky and spilled more soft moans.

Jay wait no moment. He inserted his fingers under her panty and made circles over the delicate flesh of Mian. Jay lowered his head, licking every inch of Mian's skin till his tongue reached the upper lining of Mian's panty. He felt a knot in his throat as his desire for a woman greatly increased. Her skin felt warm as Jay inserted his tongue under panty and bit the lining and pulled them down slowly till he was able to whisk it out from her legs. Feeling the ache of his tensed muscles, Jay made Mian spread her legs more, enough for Jay's body to get in between her back. Mian responded by grabbing Jay's thigh making them connected next to each other without an inch distance. Jay pushed her to the wall and anchored his left hand across Mian's right chest while his right hand is continuously making circles at Mian's delicate flesh. "Push some more and make it hard. Harder!"

Mian's desire for more sent some adrenaline to Jay's erect muscle. "I will lie flat on the floor Mian." Jay summoned Mian to slowly move down to a sitting position as he continuously pushes harder and harder and harder. Jay is lying flat on the ground while Mian is on top of him sitting, rocking with her back facing him. And Jay pulled her legs even wider and noticing how beautifully they are connected in front of a wide glass mirror. Seeing themselves sensually connected drove Mian crazy. "Can I drive?" "No! I want to push some more Mian." Mian couldn't wait. She holds Jay's thighs and makes them still and she started pushing herself up, down, forward, and backward. She made it slow and easy at first yet when she's approaching climax she went very speedy.

"Hold it!" Jay shouted. "I'm almost there too." Feeling the intensity of Mian's momentum Jay holds Mian's both flank and shifted her to a prone position. Jay saw the most beautiful site in the world as Mian is facing down and her hips are elevated. Feeling the desire swell under her stomach, Jay thrust deeply inside of her and feel the heaven over his erect muscles. He wanted to treat her more but the building climax is unstoppable that he held his breath. Mian rewarded him by pushing her back harder just as Jay released some explosive waves inside of her one after the other and sheered pleasures poured from him to her. It took them minutes before their breathing slowed back to normal and their heart beats rested in pieces.

After they satisfied each other, they both promised to love each other as friends and to help each other to find better happiness.

Few days later, Jay heard some good news from his father after knowing that his father was successful in pursuing Naayi and his Dad added that Naayi's family set a date for them to meet and to commence with a wedding.

Happiness couldn't be painted over Jay's face. After all love conquers every trials that he went into. Meanwhile, Mian felt rewarded upon hearing the upcoming marriage of Jay and all her guilt feelings were replaced with happiness knowing the only man she loves is now truly happy with someone whom he really loves as well.

On The Broken Wings of Love

The school bus driver of Amistadian's university was waiting patiently for the student-nurses to step into the bus and depart for Jimalalud, one of the most remote towns of the Philippines. Rosita, a senior student, was the last one to step into the bus after her boyfriend gave her a big hug and a kiss and waved goodbye. Rosita smiled as she filled her mind with memories of her boyfriend. Rosita was also full of anticipation for her first community duty as a student nurse, and she almost missed her chair as she settled down in the bus.

The trip was long but worthwhile. The students enjoyed the scenery as they traveled toward the untouched beauty of Jimalalud. Each student was introduced to their patient after they stepped down from the bus.

"I'm Rosita, your student-nurse," Rosita gladly introduced herself and explained the course of her stay.

"I'm Helen," came a slow voice reply.

Helen's house was situated in the innermost part of the town. The tall trees hid the house from the street. The variety of banana plants and papayas were scattered all over—a mini-plantation of some sort—yet it was obvious that those plants were not cared for. Bushes grew taller as if they were having a competition with the rest of the weeds and other plants around. A typical local rural house was Helen's. The nipa roof and the bamboo wall spoke of generation's of handmade creativity.

Rosita started her assessment with Helen right away. She asked Helen about basic information. "Husband?" "Helen repeated the last word of Rosita. "Yes, your husband. Tell me about your husband," Rosita repeated." "Oh, my husband!" Helen said. Rosita saw the sudden change in Helen's face. Helen became cheerful, talkative, and was proud of her husband. "He's a loving one, responsible, and caring for the kids." Helen continued that her husband was hardworking and always brought food when he got home from work. Helen's husband spent much time with their kids, played with them, and even cooked for them.

"Wow." Rosita was amazed and voiced that she wanted to marry her boyfriend if he was as good as Helen's.

"Could I take your blood pressure?" Rosita asked Helen. Rosita took Helen's left arm. Helen seemed nervous at first, but offered her left arm.

"What are these blue marks?" Rosita asked.

"Ahhh, I just had a fall this morning."

"They all look old to me, Helen. Where did you fall from?"

Helen couldn't give a direct answer. She paced around, held her head up and said, "Just an accident you know. When you get kids, you'll find out." Helen showed a teasing smile.

Rosita didn't last very long. She bid farewell to Helen and promised her to pay some visits for the rest of the month.

Rosita walked towards where the school bus was parked when she recalled what she saw on Helen's left arm. Those were old bruises, I'm certain, she said to herself. But that superimposed redness on her cheek was fresh and it looked like a slap, she said as she felt her pulse jump in doubt. It couldn't be, Helen claimed that her husband loves her so much, Rosita murmured in her mind and sighed.

Days and days passed. Rosita brought present for Helen and for her kids each visit: fruits, clothes, and some foods. Her compassion for Helen made a closer relationship to both of them—they became close friends. At this point, Helen became an active talker. Helen started talking about herself, kids, and her husband. "Rosita, it is not really easy to take care of kids especially when you have a husband."

"Especially when you have a husband?" Rosita asked.

"Well you know, kids and husband at the same time you know."

KNOCK. KNOCK. "Helen com'on. Open it!" A strong voice was steaming from the door like a voice of a coach in a boxing match. Rosita saw Helen pulled herself from a sitting position and opened their bamboo door that was hooked to a metal chain which kept the door locked the whole day when Helen's husband was away.

Rosita said she'd to help Helen but Helen insisted that it was her husband. Rosita felt the responsibility of a wife when Helen picked up a towel and moved with long stretch to open the door. Rosita's mind was wondering that to be a wife means you have to give your husband a welcome hug, wipe his wet body with a towel, and wash his feet with the water that was prepared next to the door's step—as Helen did to her husband.

"Who is this stranger, Helen?" Rosita felt panicky when she heard the screeching voice of a man standing in front of her. "Didn't I tell you not to have anybody in when I'm not home?" the voice continued to peel Rosita's ears." "Calm down, please. She's nice, a student-nurse," Helen's voice reassured Rosita of safety.

Rosita was introduced by Helen to her husband.

"Nice to meet you, Sir. I'm Rosita."

Rosita didn't hear anything. He saw Miguel walked to the kitchen when Helen was busy fixing the towel and the water. "Food! Helen food!" Rosita heard Miguel yell at the top of his voice. "Rosita noted some tears from Helen's eyes as she replied to Miguel with shaking lips: "Everything is on the table, Miguel, just open it." "Helen!!!" Miguel's voice almost pulled down the clock from the wall.

Rosita could no longer hold her increasing emotions. She was about to approach Miguel when she noticed the kids at the corner literally shaking. She went to the kids instead.

The kitchen was filled with raging voices 'til silence came to the house after Miguel satisfied his hunger. Helen did the dishes and was apologetic to Rosita.

"I'm so sorry."

"No you're not. You have to stop this."

"I couldn't. He's my husband."

"He's not acting as one."

"We made a vow—for better or for worse. And this is the worse part."

Rosita shook her head in disbelief. She went back to the bus and promised Helen that she would visit her before Christmas comes.

Rosita felt guilty by leaving Helen in that condition. She was not certain if Miguel would not hurt Helen this time. Rosita wanted to finish her school work fast in order for her to visit Helen in earnest.

Two days later, Rosita finished her school work. She shopped for food and gifts for Helen's kids. She was worried about them. Something could have happened to Helen, she said.

It was seven days before Christmas Eve, but Rosita could not see any sign of life at Helen's house: no Christmas lights, no Christmas décor, and no lantern. As Rosita reached Helen's house, she saw the piles of brown leaves scattered all over the ground. There were flowers at the pathway but they were thin and dry. Papayas and banana plants were all over the place but were dying as well; their leaves were hanging to the ground and were fully brown. Bushes and weeds also growing there.

KNOCK. KNOCK. Rosita waited patiently for the door to click.
KNOCK. KNOCK. She knocked again after few minutes of waiting.
Her chest started to feel heavy when the door was not opened. "Helen, I
know you're locked up inside. Please open this door." Still the door was not
opened.

Rosita took a chance. She noticed that one of the papaya plants was
close to a rear window of the house. She pulled one banana leaf and used
it as a rope to pull the papaya branch closer to the window. She was able
to connect the papaya branch to the window. She climbed up and slowly
pushed herself to the window when the branch broke, and she dropped
but luckily her left hand was able to grab the edge of the window and she
was hanging by the window. Slowly she pulled herself up and pushed the
window open. She finally got into the house.

Rosita allowed herself to get some air while she sat at a corner just in
front of the window. Suddenly she heard a weak voice. She scanned the
house and her pulse quickened when she saw Helen by the door holding
the doorknob. Yet Helen was pale and breathless. Rosita ran to Helen.

Helen's breath couldn't reach her nostrils and her pulse was hard to
locate. Rosita called for help. Helen was rushed to Bindoy's Community
Hospital.

Rosita saw how the medical team responded to Helen's condition. She
looked for a place and sat down, pressing her body against the wall and said
some prayers for Helen. Rosita went to sleep.

"Excuse me, are you related to Helen Olis? Nurse Jacqueline asked.
Rosita woke up from her deep sleep and didn't know what exactly was
happening at the moment. "Yes, could I help you?" Rosita asked nurse
Jacqueline instead.

"I'm sorry Miss. I'm Jacqueline, the nurse-in-charge of Helen Olis."

"How is she?"

"I can discuss information only with her relatives."

"I'm her younger sister," Rosita lied.

She suffered from severe dehydration and multiple injuries. She had a
history of Pneumonia and Chronic Renal Failure which complicates her
condition and almost leading her to coma. But she is alert now and her
general condition is stable."

"Thank God and thank you so much, Ms. Jacqueline—I really
appreciate your immediate attention to Helen."

Rosita eyed nurse Jacqueline as she walked in the hallway. Rosita
walked into Helen's room. She opened the door but didn't allow any noise

to disrupt Helen from her sleep. She found Helen on the bed with a tube connected from a big green tank with a gauge towards her nose. Another medium sized tube was attached to her mouth from a machine enclosed in a glass tube that had a cylinder which moved up and down as Helen breathed. A piece of small wire was attached to Helen's small right finger which was connected to a monitor and showing numbers on a screen and was beeping continuously.

Rosita kissed Helen's forehead and whispered that she would be back in a few days.

It was a humid afternoon three days later when Rosita went to visit Helen. She had so many questions needed to be answered. Electric fans were at every corner of the hospital at high speed but sweat continued to drip from Rosita's body.

KNOCK. KNOCK. Rosita went into the room after Helen invited her in. Rosita noticed the difference in Helen. Helen had gained some weight and was chattier. Rosita took the chance of asking Helen, "What happened on that day I found you half alive?"

Helen enumerated her story. Rosita found out from Helen that Miguel was mad at having a stranger in the house. After Rosita left that evening, Miguel beat Helen heavily and pulled her hair, slapped her face, punched her side, and finally hit her head using a wooden chair that made Helen unconscious. Because of too much fear, Miguel took the kids and ran.

"Are you not sad Miguel took your kids to nowhere?"

"I was glad instead."

"Whattttt? That's strange."

"They were not my kids."

Rosita learned that when Helen and Miguel got married, Monyita, a rich daughter of a politician of their town, felt in-love with Miguel. Monyita forced Miguel into an affair with an exchange of money and a well-off life.

"And you allowed that?"

"Miguel threatened to leave me, and I love him. I wanted him with me," Helen said.

Rosita felt surging pulses as Helen continued her story. Rosita's face was red in knowing that oftentimes Miguel and Monyita had their love affair in Helen's house. Rosita closed her eyes as she could feel the pain of Helen hearing raunchy voices echoing in her house.

"I would have killed them if I were you," Rosita said.

"I couldn't. I was pregnant at that time."

"You told me the kids were not yours."

"Yes. Mine was gone."

Rosita learned from Helen that Monyita knew about Helen's pregnancy and was jealous and was worried that Miguel might leave her. Monyita asked Miguel to abort Helen's baby; otherwise Miguel would lose all that he was enjoying—money, cars, and the big house in their town. Miguel then intentionally beat Helen to abort their baby. Miguel was successful.

"So those kids?" Rosita asked.

"They were Miguel's and Monyita's."

"Jesus Christ. And you took good care of them?"

"Out of too much love, yes."

"You got no plan of filing a case against Miguel?"

"I just did."

Rosita found out that Helen filed a case against Miguel and Monyita through the help of the government agency that protects the rights of women. However, Miguel and Monyita were nowhere to be found. The villagers believed they ran away.

Rosita satisfied herself with the information she got from Helen. Rosita searched for a shelter while Helen was recuperating. Rosita left Helen at the hospital but promised her that she would bring Helen to her new home.

Helen's story kept boggling in Rosita's mind so much so a reason that she failed to notice a text message from her boyfriend. Rosita went home and started scanning the yellow pages for apartments for rent.

TOT. TOT. TOT. A doorbell interrupted Rosita from her search. "Oh hi sweetie," Rosita's boyfriend greeted her with anticipations the moment she opened the door, yet Rosita didn't respond to him.

"Something's wrong?" her boyfriend asked.

"Nothing. I just realized that men were not good to keep in a woman's life."

"Whattttttttttttttttt?"

Rosita told her boyfriend of Helen's story, after which she broke up with her boyfriend without a second thought.

After two days, Rosita helped Helen file a formal complaint against Miguel in the lower court. And Rosita finally brought Helen to her new home.

"No more men," both said, raising their voices.

"No more men. No more men."

Romeo and Juliet Sex Scandal

Romeo has just finished the last of his classes for the day and was looking forward to going home, getting a shower over his scraggy body, and fixing himself his favorite dinner—a warm plate of shrimp broccoli. His brain was engrossed with things to do as he jumped off from his mini Cooper. "Ahhhhh, maybe a shower first will do," he said and started walking into the house like his first day of school just begun. He was about to squeeze the key into the door knob when he saw two shadows moving on the dark window glass. He figured they were his parents in the living room and were engaged in a deep conversation, a serious one. He sneaked and tried to interpret every single sound that would escape from the window's crevice.

"Did you go to the club?" Romeo's mom asked his dad who was seated next to her.

"Club? What is that? I have no idea what a club is," Romeo's dad said and sipped his cup of coffee and turned the television on.

"Someone told me you went and watched Juliet's show," she replied and turned the television off.

"I love only you. Is Juliet your name?" he answered quickly and picked up the television remote and placed it to his mouth instead of the cup of coffee.

"Crap!" she said and kicked the chair hard in front of her.

The most lucid sound Romeo could hear was "Juliet." His heart started to jump in turmoil but tried to remain unruffled. He then proceeded to enter the room. As he turned the door knob it clicked. His parents noticed the door slowly open and they pretended to be watching a movie, but the television was off. They were silent. Romeo approached them.

"Mom, Dad. Juliet? I know her. She's a very desirable and fabulous girl. Where did you meet her Dad? Romeo asked.

"In the club," his mom said, staring straight at the blank TV screen.

"No. In the mall," his dad said.

"What? Look at that! You told me you didn't know her and now you dated her?" his mom shrieked. "Mom, Dad is just playing with you. He loves you, right Daddy? Now why don't you two take a shower because you both stink," he added teasingly.

Romeo turned his back and walked to his room. "I know Dad didn't meet Juliet. I'm positive," Romeo said to himself and scratched his head. He took his key to open his room but it took time for him to open the door, missing the lock several times. He put his back pack into the closet and left. He went to his aunt to learn the whereabouts of his dad. His father always told his aunt where he was going. They were that close.

TOT!TOT! Romeo's car made some noise as he was approaching his aunt's house. They talked and his aunt told Romeo that his dad went to the club to watch Juliet's show.

"What? So he saw Juliet? he asked.

"I guess so. That's what your dad wants to see, Juliet. Is there a problem with that?"

"This is horrible."

"Hey, Romeo" called his friend, Lexus, who was passing in front of his aunt's house, interrupting their conversation. Lexus was dressed as if he was ready to go to a party.

"How's my brother?" Lexus yelled and waved his hand as he was approaching Romeo who was walking together with her aunt to meet him at the gate.

"Brother?" Romeo's aunt said with upright eyebrow and was looking straight at Romeo.

"I'm okay my brother," Romeo said in a big voice and gave Lexus a welcome hug while his other fingers pinched his aunt's side.

"Ouch, God damnit!"

"Anything wrong?" Lexus asked.

"No brother. I'll see you at the show tonight."

"Great."

Lexus left.

Later that night, close to ten o'clock, Romeo was dressed in his tight white top and straight jeans, ready to go to the Golden Touch club thrilled with anticipation. He parked his car at the back of the club, and walked with small steps and was scanning around as he approached the club. He opened the club's door, flashing lights in bright colors captured his eyes, and air bubbles from everywhere flew into the air. Everybody was dancing. His eyes scanned the room looking for a place to sit. The dim light and the dancing crowd made it harder for him to find a spot. Finally, in a hidden corner next to the stage floor, he saw a spot with a man seated at a table.

"Sir, a glass of Martini please," Romeo addressed the waiter.

"Romeo!"

"Dad? You're here?"

Romeo felt running horses on his chest. His cheek felt like ice and his knees trembled but he tried to talk as calm as he could.

"Dad, you're not supposed to be here. This place is for young unmarried guys. Let's go home, otherwise, I'm going to tell Mom."

His father was quiet as the two of them rode home. As they stepped out from Romeo's car Romeo grabbed his dad's hand and pulled him inside the house. They were moving into the house like a bomb squad trying to detonate a bomb that is about to explode in seconds. "Dad, I'll get some water from the kitchen." His dad wanted to talk to Romeo but Romeo eluded without notice. Romeo was nowhere to be found. His dad didn't notice him leaving through the back door. Romeo drove as fast as he could back to the club. He was late and he promised Lexus to meet him there before the show started. As he approached the club he heard the crowd yelling, "JULIET, JULIET."

"I should be there now," he said.

The show is about to start. The dazzling lights went off. And the crowd shouted more, "JULIET, JULIET . . . ." A few minutes passed and Juliet still did not emerge from behind the stage curtains. Juliet's boyfriend, Lexus, who was in the crowd, got worried.

"Juliet should be here by now," Lexus said to himself.

Lexus lifted his phone and tried to contact Juliet. "Out of coverage area." He shifted his weight on the floor and moved towards the exit to find Juliet. He opened the door and realized that the person running toward the club was Juliet. He sighed, felt relief and met Juliet before she reached the door.

"I'm glad you made it!" he said.

"Emergency."

"And those sneakers?" he asked.

Juliet had no time to explain. She seized Lexus' hand and went directly to the dressing room. Juliet went inside to change and went on the stage to perform. "How come she had Romeo's sneakers on?" Lexus asked himself as he walked to his chair to sit and watched Juliet perform.

The show was perfect as expected. The crowd was yelling for more. Juliet's svelte body, fair skin, and raunchy movements invited more customers and suitors like Romeo's dad.

"That was great Juliet! I'm so proud you are my girlfriend," Lexus said.

"I'll do more next time if you pick me up."

"Sure. By the way, I haven't seen Romeo. He told me he would come to watch your show."

"He's home. We had an emergency that's why I took his sneakers by mistake."

"Oh I see. I'm sorry to hear that."

Their conversation went on as they drove home. They approached Juliet's apartment. The lights were out and silence surrounded the four corners of the house. Romeo made a stop few steps away from Juliet's apartment. They both stepped out from the car and walked. Then Juliet paced gracefully towards her apartment door herself. She looked back at Lexus and waved "good-bye."

Lexus started to walk towards his car. He put on his black, leather jacket. He lit his cigar and whistled as he walked away from Juliet's house.

"Hey brother, I'm sorry." Someone called him from a distance. Lexus turned his head to where the voice came from and noticed a shadow by the window.

"Is that you Romeo?" he asked.

"Ah huh."

He shook his head. "You didn't show up brother. It was fun. But it's okay."

"I'm sorry. Emergency."

"You should have seen Juliet perform."

"Was she great?"

"Oh yes she was. I loved it and I love her so much."

"Nice to hear that brother, I'll make it next time. I promise."

"No more emergency, huh? Bye."

Romeo waved good bye. Romeo walked toward the door to switch off the light when Lexus suddenly yelled from the outside, "Is that Juliet's outfit? The one hanging behind your door?"

"No. Of course not," Romeo said.

"But that lei is mine. I gave it to her during the show."

"Oh yeah. I'm sorry. Yes I remembered. She stopped by the apartment just few minutes ago and handed her dress to me to have it pressed by tomorrow.

Romeo ran to the door. He removed the dress, turned off the light and said, "I'll see you tomorrow brother. Bye." The lights were gone.

Lexus scratched his head in wonder.

The next morning, Romeo was in a deep sleep. His dad could hear him snore from the open door of his room. His dad walked in to see Romeo.

"Look at my son. This built muscle, wide chest, and broad shoulders. I used to have them when I was younger. I'm glad my son is just like me."

He paced the room. Pulled up the shade and opened the window. He recalled how Romeo grew up in this room. Memories were playing in his head. He was about to leave the room when something fell from the closet.

"A doll? Why would he keep this old doll? He wondered.

"What use could it possibly have? He picked up the doll and placed it back on top of the closet, and found one more thing.

Angered his father screamed, "What is this, Romeo get up!" His voice roared like a lion.

"Dad."

"Why do you have this red Anne Klein watch? I gave it to the guard at the club for Juliet just two weeks ago."

Romeo was still dozing. He didn't clearly understand what his dad said. He stretched his arms, yawned, and squeezed his eyes.

"Good morning dad." He went back to bed.

"For Chrissake pull yourself up and talk to me!"

The loud voice pinched Romeo's ears like needles.

"Dad, what's wrong with you? Leave me alone, please."

"What's this? And this? And this?" his dad asking him while pointing to Romeo's closet. He found a make-up kit. Bikinis. Lady's perfume. And . . . He lifted the red dress on the floor.

"Romeo, this was the outfit that Juliet wore at last night's show. Explain this to me!"

Romeo was teetering. His nervous voice wheezed as a he said, "I'm sorry dad. Yes, I'm—I'm Juliet."

"Oh my God, this is a curse from hell!"

Romeo pulled his body up, and sat against the wall. He put his arms across his knees and braced his chin as he tried to hold his tears from flowing.

"Dad, I just wanted to be me. I wanted to exist."

"But son!"

"Yes Dad. I knew you wouldn't like me, but I'm your son, not your belonging. I have my own life, and my own dreams. But I suppressed my happiness because I love you. Do you know how hard it is to be a man? To be the way you want me to be?

"Because you are a man and not a Juliet!" his father shouted.

"Yes. I'm a man. But I can't act like a man. It's so hard to pretend each day. Walk like a soldier when I want to walk like my mom. Look at my hair, it's so short when I wanted it long and curly. Dad, please. I wanted to be happy like you are. If you're happy to have a son then let me be happy as I am. You have your life and I have mine to live. I thank you for the life you gave but I have to live my life the way I want it to be, not yours."

Romeo's dad was tight-lipped. He wanted to show his anger but he was aware of Romeo's acute suffering.

"Look at this mirror Dad."

Romeo handed him a mirror. Romeo pointed out that this mirror was the witness of how he suffered.

"I look at this mirror to make sure that I am Romeo when I face you Dad, my friends, and schoolmates. Then when I'm alone I look in the same mirror and I see Juliet, the real me who I am not allowed to be, and I am a downcast and unfulfilled."

It took time for Romeo's dad to make a comment. He paced around the room, clinched his fists, and shook his head. Then finally he offered a soft voice. "I love you my son, and I'm sorry. Whether you are a Romeo or a Juliet, I will love you."

"But I bet you love the fantasy of Juliet more?"

"Don't tell your mom about it. Don't even try to tell her that Juliet is sexier and prettier than she is."

Laughter shattered the silence of the room as Romeo and his dad teased about Juliet.

"What's your plan about your boyfriend?"

"I'll see him tonight Dad. Don't worry, I'll handle this with care."

The two had some drinks together. Both enjoyed the moment they had accepted their differences. When evening came, Romeo excused himself. "Dad, I'll see Lexus." Romeo prepared himself to meet Lexus in the club to tell him about Juliet. Romeo wore his regular dress, white top, straight jeans, and his favorite Mizuno white sneakers.

Romeo drove his car at 40mph. He made some stops along the way, then drove then stopped again. Finally he drove continuously and reached the Golden Touch club before ten in the evening. He parked this time at the front of the club. "I can do this," he said to himself, and watched the crowd outside the club.

People were in the line at the club's entrance door with their tickets in hand. Some were rowdy and others smoked and drank beer. The atmosphere was charged with anticipation. Romeo recognized Lexus right away who was in the line.

"Brother," Romeo called Lexus with an undertone from a distance.

"Come here brother, squeeze yourself into the line," Lexus said.

"Wait brother, I need you just a while. It's important. Please follow me at the bayside."

"This must be an emergency brother."

"Yes. Emergency and I need to act faster than 911."

Lexus pulled himself out of the line and followed Romeo towards the bayside just across the street from the club. Lexus can see the weight on Romeo's shoulders.

"This must be really serious," Lexus said to himself.

The water around bayside made gentle crashing sounds as they hit the shore. The night lights converged in the water and mirrored diamond-like sparkles. Lovers were walking around taking their most quite time together. There were few empty benches at different corners eyeing for esoteric individual to enjoy the splendid beauty of bayside.

"Have a seat beside me Lexus, this bench is wide enough for both of us."

The two sat next to each other. Lexus started talking about Juliet and how he love her so much. Romeo offered nothing but silence.

"Tell me Romeo."

"You love Juliet, right?"

"I'm positive."

"And you're willing to accept anything about her?"

"Ofcourse. She's an entertainer and I'm proud of that. I'm not ashamed because I love her."

"And if she's just a fantasy?"

"A fantasy?"

"Yes. A fantasy like Cinderella, not a real one."

Lexus stood up, turned his back and walked away. Romeo followed him quickly and held his hands.

"That touch," Lexus said. "It's Juliet's!"

"Yes, it's Juliet's. I knew you would recognize the caress even if you didn't see her face."

Lexus broke from his hold and pushed him back. Then he punched the air with his fist.

"But how? I thought you were related?"

"We're not. We're one."

"But why did you lie so long?"

"Because I was afraid to lose you and I realized the relationship was wrong."

Romeo explained that he used the façade of being a Romeo because this is what others expect of him. He confided that his own personal happiness was realized only when he was Juliet.

"Romeo, I can continue with my fantasy."

"It is wrong. I would dearly love to share that fantasy with you for a few hours each night, but it is still wrong."

"But nobody knows or has to know."

Romeo continued to explain to Lexus that everybody grows old and fantasies grow old faster than age. Once our legs can no longer hold us upright, we need somebody to give us a hand—a son, daughter, a family. Even if our hearts and minds and our body disagree with each other still we need a hand to lift us up. But we can't achieve this not unless we stay as we were naturally created. When you were created in the image of a man it is not fitting to be clothed in a woman's dress.

Lexus got the idea. Although it was not easy for him to break up with Juliet but he knew too that their relationship is wrong. A man needs a woman not another man. Lexus held Romeo's hands and kissed them one last time, letting go of his fantasies over the beautiful Juliet.

"Juliet! Juliet!Juliet!"

They heard the crowd from the Golden Touch club shouting Juliet's name as the clock touched ten.

"Juliet? Who's performing now Juliet, I mean Romeo?" Lexus asked, puzzled.

Romeo laughed. "My aunt. That's her fantasy—to be a Juliet. She's happy with it."

"Well, no one can tell who's the real Juliet is since Juliet always performs with her mask on."

The Final Revelation

(Is Jesus Christ a Man or a True God?)

A strong strike from a sword hit the neck of another unknown victim. The head dropped and rolled to the ground while blood gushed out from the severed neck. And a bloke, from nowhere, in a long black suit came running and began to inspect the whole body from arms, front, back, and feet—looking for something very important.

"Stop!" Ms. Jo Lu, a Romanian detective, shouted at the bloke as she stepped down from her V8-engine vehicle. But the bloke was gone, as if he had vanished into thin air.

Jo was frustrated.

She believed the bloke had something to do with all the mysterious killings here in New York City for the past few days.

Sirens were wailing from a distance.

Meanwhile, police officers examined the body. They noted a distinct pattern: the head was cut from behind, both palms and feet had a hole measuring 1c.m. in diameter, there was a stab wound to the right ride side of the abdomen, and an inverted cross was crudely drawn on the man's forehead.

"This is how exactly Christians were persecuted at the cross," Jo claimed. She added that the inverted cross implied that the killer/killers were the antichrist.

"Ms. Jo," an officer interrupted from behind bringing the latest report connected to the killings. Jo held her breath as she read the report. "All of them . . . Church of Corinth, Thessalonians . . . , these victims have a blood line related to the priest . . . where St. Paul last visited." Who could be next? she wondered.

BEEP BEEP! It was her phone, a voice mail from an unknown caller—the man from the crime scene! After hearing the address that he gave on his message, she quickly packed her gear and left the scene. She knew exactly where the place was.

Jo already had her 908 Smith & Wesson handgun drawn out even before the elevator door opened to the floor. The floor was deserted and quiet, and all she could hear was the loud thumping of her heart. She slowly entered the room, where she found the man gripping a Roman Gladius sword, kneeling on the floor. Her mind confirmed that the man in front of her was the killer.

"Killing me now will not help you solve those crimes," he said quietly as he stared at the floor, gripping the sword so tightly that his knuckles were white. "I was the one who called you. I can help you solve those crimes."

"Help me?" Jo asked, pointing her gun at him.

"I'm Cyrus, the messenger appointed by God to gather His people from the East to the West. And because of this, they are trying to kill me."

"They?"

"The antichrist, they who built their Church in 1914 in the Philippines claiming they were the seed of the East."

"What makes you think that their claim is untrue?" Jo asked.

"For I am the messenger appointed by God mentioned in the book of Isaiah, and Timothy knew that God's church cannot be in Asia for Asia turned away from God.

As Cyrus continued to explain everything to Jo, the sound of gunfire echoed from a distance, cracking the window and nearly hitting Cyrus. He managed to roll over and quickly pulled Jo for cover. He stopped Jo from calling for back-up. Instead, he turned off the light, and they both crawled towards a hidden exit door and jumped into his get-away car.

After more than four hours on the road, Jo found out that she was about to discover a very important Christian secret never told before. Cyrus turned the car onto a dirt road and stopped his car by a house surrounded by tall pine trees, and the two hurried inside.

Inside the house, Cyrus led Jo to a bookshelf that housed numerous ancient scrolls. She also noticed an old man, age unknown, praying at the altar. Moments later, Cyrus joined him and the two had a long quiet conversation that Jo assumed to be in Hebrew.

Jo asked Cyrus for an interpretation the moment Cyrus took his place by her side.

"There is only one true Christian Church—the Church of Christ," Cyrus began.

"Well, that is recorded in the book of Matthew," Jo agreed. But she was still confused and skeptical.

"Christ's church will not perish so no one can claim that His church was apostatized. Otherwise, Christ is a liar," Cyrus continued.

According to Cyrus, God always gives an example. From the Old Testament, Noah built an ark to save his family. This is the same with Christ. He built the one true church, His Church and only the members of this Church have the assurance of salvation.

"But the final revelation is this," Cyrus said, who suddenly sounded tired and weak.

With eagerness, Jo asked, "What is it?"

"**Christ is the TRUE GREAT GOD AND ALMIGHTY**," Cyrus said.

He looked to the old man and said, "He is the proof for he is a descendant of St. John, the one who wrote the Book of Revelation, and I'm going to quote the following verses," Cyrus continued.

Cyrus began to read, "Behold, he is coming amid the clouds and every eye shall see him, and they also which pierced him. I am the Alpha and Omega says the Lord, which is, and which was, and which is to come, the Almighty. Holy, holy, holy is the Lord God Almighty, who was, and who is, and who is to come."

Jo felt the spirit as she heard this Revelation.

"Cyrus, I need to transfer these to my laptop. I'll get it from the car so that I can present these to the proper authorities soon." She could not help herself from mumbling the verses she heard inside the house to herself: "Seen from the clouds. Seen by those who pierced Him. Which is, and which was, and which is to come, the Almighty. The God Almighty. "Jesus Christ, why now? Why reveal all of these to me now?" she asked no one in particular, exasperated.

She was still thinking about the verses that Cyrus said as she approached her car and fumbled with the keys. Suddenly, a loud explosion pushed her against the car door, slamming her chest against the hard, tinted windows. Looking back, she could see that the house was a burning inferno of flames and black smoke that curled angrily towards the sky.

Coughing in pain from the slam against the car, she made her way back to the house, shielding her face from the heat that seemed to reach out even to the driveway. Suddenly, a second explosion propelled her to the ground, just a few meters from the doorway of the house which was now engulfed in flames. Before passing out she could make out the glowing outline of her car, with the flames dancing menacingly out the broken windows.

"Ms. Jo Lu!" The sounds seemed to be far-away echoes. Jo opened her eyes. Her tongue felt thick and she could taste the smoke in her mouth. A paramedic was leaning over her, shining a flashlight over her eyes. She was inside the ambulance. Outside, firemen were dousing the house with water. Sirens of responding cop cars were slowly getting louder.

"Good, she's awake." A man was peering into the ambulance. From the gray overcoat to the haggard, unshaven look, Jo could tell that the man was a detective. "Can I talk to her?"

The paramedic looked at Jo, as if asking her the question. She nodded, feeling the pain in her neck as she did so.

"Are there any people inside the house?" he asked, climbing inside the ambulance. But before she could answer, a fireman, his face black with soot, peered inside the ambulance.

"Detective, no one's inside. It's clear. Could be she was the only one there."

Jo felt a lump in her throat. She could not speak. She was not sure if Cyrus and the old man survived from the explosion or they both died protecting the Christian's faith. But she was sure that the world needed to know about Cyrus and the old man and about the things that they revealed to her.

"Whenever I'm ready, I'm going to tell the world about the TRUTH!" she vowed, before falling back into unconsciousness.

Voices Of The Unborn

It was a warm October evening when Jimboy decided to pick Tata up for an adventure later that night. Both decided to visit Bogo cemetery—the local cemetery known for its ghost haunting.

They stepped-down from their bikes upon reaching the closed cemetery gates. The setting sun made the shadows of the lofty acacia trees that bowed over the graves dance like sinister disembodied ghosts. The whistling soft breeze inside Bogo swayed the undulating grasses along the pathway. Jimboy and Tata, as they walked through, heard the different noise from insects and other creatures. But Tata knew he heard something else. "Is someone weeping?" he asked, unable to contain his fear.

The weeping sound became more distinct as they drew nearer towards the "Big Cross" which stood at the heart of the cemetery. A young lady was standing still at the foot of the cross surrounded by several lighted candles. The whole place was so quite that they could hear the murmurs of the lady even from where they stood. William and Tata stepped closer.

"Lola, is this you?" Jimboy asked.

"Yah this is me Jimboy."

"By yourself?"

"Yes. I've been here since an hour ago."

"Excuse me Lola and Jimboy" Tata interrupted. I need to move the bikes. It's getting late. I'll come back soon," he said as he walked away.

"I need your help again, Jimboy," Lola said.

"Again?"

"You're hesitant now? You hit the lotto so you don't need money?"

"It's not that, but I have other reasons to consider now."

"And that must include Tata's presence which is not supposed to be!" Lola's raised voice broke through the silence of the cemetery.

From a distance, Tata was slowly returning. He walked slowly as he wondered by Lola's lighting candles in the section of the cemetery marked

UNBORN CHILDREN. "Jimboy brought me here for a reason," he said to himself. "The place is humored to be inhabited by ghosts. The date is October 31st. It's six in the evening. Nobody is valiant to come here at this hour except . . ." Tata stopped his ramblings and started screaming in alarm when he accidentally stepped-over a pile-of-bones that were not fully covered with dirt.

"We need to go home now idiots!" Tata shouted at Lola and Jimboy.

They hurried home.

Jimboy dropped Lola off first. "I need it by tomorrow no matter what. Same time. Same place," she said as she bid him goodbye. Without a word Jimboy left her and proceeded to drop Tata off at his house.

Tata felt confused about what happened. While the two were entering Bogo, earlier, Jimboy had left him alone. Tata found him in a secluded portion of the cemetery fixing something. Jimboy was standing inside what looked like a big sepulcher which can accommodate about five people. The entire area was surrounded with several piles-of-dirt approximately two feet by one foot in measure, and it was easily hidden from view by the grass that grew around it. Tata had no idea what would bring Jimboy to that place. Unable to endure his curiosity, Tata decided to call his friend.

"He's not home," Jimboy's daughter said when she picked up the phone.

"Not home? Where is he?" Tata asked.

"He said that he'll be at the park," his daughter replied.

Jimboy was at the city's park—sitting in one of the benches so that he could be alone with his thoughts.

"Can I refuse Lola?" he asked himself over and over again, almost chanting to himself.

Jimboy's father is in the hospital and has been in a coma for two years.

Meanwhile, his only daughter is in her last year of law school. For years Jimboy pretended that he could afford all finances through his business, which was rapidly failing. The sad reality was that he was dependent on his clients, especially on Lola. It was she who supported him with large amounts of money every month so he and his family could financially stay afloat. But Jimboy knew that his situation was bleak. Not knowing what to do, he passed by the church on his way home and said his prayers.

He went home late that night and went straight to his bed. Around three in the morning, he heard shrill voices coming from nowhere. He got up, got dressed, and was surprised to find children playing in the yard. He was so upset that he tried to grab one of them. However, the moment he managed to catch the arm of one of the children, the arm fell off! Jimboy was shocked and could no longer breathe, all the more when around him, the rest of the children started to bleed! Their skin started to peel-off from their bones, and their intestines slithered their way out of their small bellies through large, gaping holes that were miraculously appearing before his eyes. The children's eyeballs started dropping to the ground while stared straight at him. Jimboy saw their hearts pump blood uselessly through severed arteries, while their livers boiled with the strong smell of acidic bile. The children's bodies started blue until they all collapsed, whispering in tiny, shrill voices, "Why Daddy? I should be playing by now and enjoying school as my younger sister is. I should be kissing mom but she died. She died because of you!" Jimboy, shocked and dazed, couldn't breathe. He eventually managed a feeble cry for help, which sent his daughter running to his aid.

"Dad, are you okay? You're perspiring a lot," his daughter said. "Where's your sister?" he asked. This confused her daughter, since she was an only child. "Dad, you just had a nightmare," she explained, trying desperately to calm him.

The phone rings. "Dad, it's Lola," his daughter said. "And Dad tomorrow is the deadline for my tuition fee."

"Tell her I'm coming."

Later that day, Jimboy and Lola met and did what they had to do. Jimboy promised Lola that this would be the last time. Afterwards, they both went to the Big Cross and offered candles.

A year later, on October 31st at six in the evening, Jimboy stood at the same cross in Bogo and found a lady with a young girl praying at the Big Cross. "Lola, is this you?" he asked.

"Yes, Jimboy," she replied. Meet my daughter, Lanie."

"Daughter?"

"Surprised?"

"I'm not," he replied, not knowing whether to be happy, guilty, or sad. "I was expecting her."

"You fooled me last year, Lola said. I doubted that you would do it, especially since you brought Tata along with you. I knew you won't do it. Tell me how it happened."

"I needed the money that time," Jimboy started to confess. "Badly." He started telling the story. He had no choice but to continue the abortive procedure for Lola. But his conscience wouldn't let him! To avoid killing another innocent child, he gave Lola a sleeping pill instead of the abortive pill. When Lola woke-up, Jimboy showed to her the remnants of a fetus, the fetus that he had earlier taken from the cemetery, and so she believed it was done.

From then on, the Big Cross of Bogo became a meeting place for Jimboy and Lola and others who had aborted their children.

Jimboy and Lola founded an organization against abortion and started a support group for those who had experienced an abortion. Their organization also offers free counseling and supports strong family relationships. All of these happened because they heard the "VOICES OF THE UNBORN."

Heartbeats

At a very peaceful and native town of Dyonbi, Kuya was introduced to Foto's family, his girlfriend. He met her parents, cousins, and some other relatives.

There was a big banquet served inside a huge cottage, a few minutes' drive from Dyonbi, by Foto's aunt. The patio which is overlooking the sea welcomes everyone with a chilly air from its surrounding that has lots of fruit trees. The smell of native chicken soup, grilled fresh shrimp and clamps on the table boiled the stomach of Kuya to hunger that he almost forget the tradition of Foto's family which is to pick-up everyone's right hand and put it over to his forehead and ask for a blessing. Kuya recited prayers for the memorable dinner commencement.

"I love to build a nipa hut right in this place," Kuya said to Foto as they were sitting next to each other.
"And why?" Foto asked as she is embracing Kuya and gave him a soft kiss on his lips.
"Because this place has lots of love which kidnapped my heart."

Unending young love shared by Kuya and Foto burned the night. Everyone noticed what a lovely couple they are. Their sweetness put everyone into a happy sleep.

The sunbeam wakes Kuya from a deep sleep. He got up and grabbed his digital camera and took pictures of a beautiful sun rising from the ocean. He then took pictures of Foto who is still asleep. Love melt in the lips of Kuya as he kissed each picture of his beautiful Foto.

The rest of Foto's family was busy preparing a breakfast. Meanwhile, Kuya is now teasing Foto to wake up and the two begun to share their sweetness. Even at their late twenties, love makes them feel younger like teenagers who are so playful. They start caressing each other, biting each other's arms, kicking, running after each other, and pulling each other's hair. While the lovers play, people happily take in this sight.

"They are the sweetest lovers I have ever seen in my entire life," one of Foto's aunt said.

When the long day was upon them, they returned to the beach for Kuya's celebration.

Kuya stated . . . I feel so scared Foto.
"We'll still see and call each other Kuya."
"I know but my heart just wants to be where you are."

The sunset is appearing and Kuya has to return to his city while Foto has to stay in her town, Dyonbi.

Four days later, Kuya received a text message from Foto: "Please see me at your earnest. We need to talk!"

Kuya's heart jumped with tremors. He drove fast to Foto's house and went straight to the cottage as Foto should be waiting there. He run fast but the quietness of the place made him go slow. He was burning with perspiration yet the chilly air made him cold. There was no single light at the cottage except for a few candle lanterns hanging around the patio. Kuya could not locate Foto. As he searched for her, his ears were pierced by the weeping sounds which led him to her. Kuya found Foto seated on the floor gazing aimlessly at the sea. He approached her from the back and gave her a tight embrace and kissed her by the neck, but Foto surprisingly resisted everything.

"I told you to be careful, but you were not!" Foto said almost choking her words.
"I was," Kuya claimed.

"But my aunt saw you both," Foto said.

Kuya learned that Foto's aunt saw him together with his ex-girlfriend.
"But Foto, they must understand," Kuya said.
"They would not," Foto disagreed.
"I will explain everything to them," Kuya said.
"They would not accept your reasons. They would never understand how an ex-girlfriend would still stay and live in your damn house," Foto explained.
"Not in my house! I told you that! My ex-girlfriend resides with my parent's house," Kuya shouted.
"Yes with your parent's house that is few steps away from your house and in one same compound," Foto said.
"But we are not living-in together and we broke-up for more than a year now."
"Yes more than a year, but the people around you, your neighbors, friends, and your relatives know that you were together for almost ten years and all of them prefer to have her for you than any other woman, especially your parents."

The two continue. Kuya felt bad because he is travelling in the next two days toward a far city to work.

"All I can say is that, I love you more than anyone else even more than I love my parents and family," Kuya softly said.
"If you truly love me, then we have to fight for this together," Kuya added.
Out of fear of losing Foto, Kuya holds her hands and said, "Foto, will you marry me?"
"What? Do you know what you are doing Kuya?"
"Of course I know what I'm doing. I am also scared, but if we get married . . . no one will separate us."
"Buy Kuya, I want my family to bless me, us! If we do this now, they are going to hate us forever."
"So you don't love me at all?" Kuya asked.
"I love you . . . but we need to face our problems. We need to resolve our problem. We cannot accomplish this by jumping into marriage right now," Foto explained.

Kuya was not able to convince Foto of his proposal. He went home and packed-up for the next day's travel. He was packing his bag when he saw his parents having a very lovely conversation at their living room.

"How could I talk to my parents about Foto?" he asked himself.

Kuya grows with the anticipation of speaking to his parents about Foto. Although he is hesitant to share with his parents everything in his heart, he decides to resurrect the courage to speak to them.

Kuya: hmmm, hmm, "excuse me Mom? Dad? Sorry to interrupt you both . . . but . . . I need to talk to you."

"What is it son?" his father asked.

Kuya had trouble speaking. Sweat starts to harbor his forehead and he's shaky. Kuya's voice trembles as the words come slowly out of his mouth.

"Dad, Mom I have a new girlfriend."

"What? Do you know what you are doing son?" As his father's voice escalates in tone . . . his father glares at Kuya. Kuya's father comes close to striking him.

"Calm down darling, let our son explain. He must have good reasons for this," his mom said as she held her left artificial leg down to the floor.

"But Dad, I love her and I will marry her soon and only her," Kuya said.

"You want to marry her? Why? I don't understand? Where was this woman when your mother and I almost lost our lives three years ago? Will this new girlfriend of yours feed me when my left arm suffers paralysis? Well . . . Answer me! Will she? Will she care for us?"

"Ofcourse she was not doing all those. How could she when I don't meet her yet at those times, otherwise, definitely she would do the same."

"How sure are you of this? You even don't know her that much, her character, her family, especially her personal background."

"I love her dad."

"Love wouldn't change what kind of person she is. I will contact all my friends to investigate your girl."

"Darling, you don't have to do that. Leave our son alone. Don't do what your parents did to us. You are becoming more like them," his mom said.

"What is the occupation of her parents Son?" his dad asked.

"Her mom is a physician and her father is a lawyer."

"Wow! Are you trying to improve your social status Son? Are you tired of being poor?"

"Dad, she loves me."

"Why would she love you? You have nothing! You do not have a professional title or importance status, do you?

"Tell me something . . . is this why you married my mother and not your first love?"

"Stop!" his mom weeps.

"Look at me Son, go and do whatever you want. Just don't mention that girl anymore," his mom said.

Kuya picked up his luggage and is about to leave.

"You cannot bring any other woman in this house son. Do you understand?" his dad shouted at him and Kuya banged the door.

Kuya boarded in the plane with a heavy heart.

"Oh my God," Kuya said.

He was watching a Korean movie during the flight and the movie simply reminds him of Foto and he began to cry. He covered his face with a blanket and pretended to be asleep.

"Are you okay Sir?" a flight attendant asked.

"Yes I am."

"I'm sorry; I thought I heard you crying."

"Oh no, I'm a man. I'll never do that. That's too childish."

The plane landed. Kuya went straight to his new apartment and furnished the apartment with the things he needed.

While away from Foto, Kuya has difficulty adjusting to his new environment. Every morning Kuya woke up early being troubled with so many things: family problem, job-related, and with Foto. One morning, while Kuya is preparing his food for work he experienced something strange.

"Ouch." Kuya felt some aching chest pain that he never had before. It is very unusual to him. Kuya realized that he missed Foto tremendously. Two days later, Kuya is still having same experience with his chest pain and he begun to worry. Kuya knew he was an emotional person. However, he was unaware he could feel such intense pain from just missing someone. "It's like someone is squeezing my heart from the inside and when it happens, I remember Foto," Kuya murmured to himself.

The pain that Kuya is having on his chest is occurring twice in a day—one in early morning and another similar pain in the evening. The pattern is the same and it is increasing in intensity every time it happens. Kuya felt terrible with this pain. He began to think of crazy things like killing himself. He even phoned his brother and voiced his wish to die. However, every time he calls Foto this pain simply vanish without a reason at all.

"I'm dying to see you Foto," Kuya said to Foto over the phone during one of their conversations. "I can't wait to taste again the sweetness of your kiss." And Kuya has to phone Foto every morning and evening to get relief from this mysterious pain.

Next morning, he called his mother. They had a long conversation and he mentioned to his mother regarding his chest pain.

"Where is Foto from Son?" his mother asked.

"Dyonbi."

"Son, I'm not coming to a conclusion yet that place is known for black magic and sorcery."

"Mom, you're so outdated and besides she wouldn't that to me because she loves me."

"I doubt it Son."

Later that afternoon, Kuya received a text message from his mom. Kuya phoned his mom at that instant. Kuya felt as though his heart would leap onto the floor when he heard from his mother.

"No way Mom. No way!"

Kuya just learned from his mom that Foto sought help from two sorcerers to do a spell on him. One sorcerer would inflict pain on him in the morning while the next sorcerer would do same thing in the evening. And the only relief from this pain is Foto's voice or to look at her picture. Otherwise, Kuya would lose his sanity or would jump-off from a height. Upon learning this, Kuya was so shocked of what the card-reader was telling his mom because it has truth in it. "Kuya ponders quietly to himself . . ." how many times do I consider jumping off the roof while at work?" Kuya found this alarming news hard to believe. However, his rural background instilled practical values within him. Kuya's rural roots forced him to seek a second opinion from another knowledgeable practitioner.

It was Friday at eleven at night when Kuya went to look for this lady who is known for her sorcery. Her office is in a basement. The entrance to her office looks like a big cathedral. Several figures are on the wall and few statutes of saints are on the wall too. That night, a long line of clients were waiting to see this lady. Kuya waited till 3 in the morning before he gets the chance to be seen by this lady.

"Give me your hands," the lady said. "It's positive."

Kuya is wondering what the lady was speaking of when making her odd statement. The lady recited some prayers in an unfamiliar language to Kuya. Next, the lady took a plain white paper and poured some oil on it then rub it on Kuya's forehead.

"It's a girl!" Kuya almost shouted upon looking at the figure that was printed on the plain paper after it was rubbed on his forehead. He felt terrified.

The lady explained to Kuya, that the woman cast this spell upon him, loves him too much. The woman that was printed on the paper was the one to blame for this spell. The intention of this young woman was geared toward Kuya.

Kuya remembered how she met Foto. He found her at Friendster an internet engine where you can post your pictures. Then they chatted over Yahoo Messenger, another internet engine where you can talk and see each other via a webcam on a computer. "The first time I saw you I have given my whole heart to you," Kuya remembered what he told Foto for the very first time he saw her and he knew he really love her on that very instant.

"Kuya! Kuya!" the lady shouted Kuya's name.

"Yes, I'm still here," he replied.

"Do this to save yourself."

Kuya was asked to light one pink candle everyday for 9 days. He was given a red handkerchief with some strange words on it. Then the white paper that was used on Kuya earlier was sealed in a bottle with some oil in it.

Kuya's heart was broken despite his discovery. Kuya continued to chat with Foto daily.

Since Kuya is sentimental, he enjoys sharing his stories with his friends. Although, one day a close friend shared a startling piece of information.

"I know your girl," Meonas said, Kuya's childhood friend.

Kuya is so interested on what Meonas is going to tell him. He trusted Meonas very much. The two of them exchange email messages constantly. Through Meonas influence and connections back in their city, Kuya knows that he can rely on Meonas informations. Kuya then learned from Meonas that Foto had sexual affairs with few men including in the gym where Foto practiced her Martial Arts. Some men rumored Foto as a whore. "That's enough!" Kuya shouted while reading the email messages he received. He was trying to control his emotions but he couldn't stop himself from crying. He decided to go back home to discuss things with Foto.

While Kuya is on the way home, he receives more disturbing news. One of his spies, the one he asked to look after Foto, send him a picture of Foto via email. The Photo shows Foto with a young Korean guy in a restaurant. Another spy reported to him that Foto usually jog with someone every morning, and this guy is Foto's suitor.

Kuya does not want to read his email any longer. He told his spies to stop eyeing Foto.

The plane landed at Kuya's home city.

Dyonbi remains the same after Kuya left the place few months ago. Folks are still in the corner of the street counting passing vehicles as if there's nothing else to do. Few are drinking native wine in a mini-store. Life is so simple in Dyonbi that you wouldn't recognize anyone having a problem except Kuya. His dull talks, slowed pace walk, and not touching his favorite dish would tell you he has an inevitable problem at the moment. Inorder to focus with his condition, Kuya went to visit his most trusted friend, Jacq, to confide his situation and seek advice.

Two in the afternoon. Kuya and Jacq went to a SPA saloon.

The stairs to the SPA room was wide and long which would give you time to empty your thoughts as you climb the stairs. There were several red Chinese lanterns in the ceiling to calm your eyes. An instrumental music is continuously playing throughout the whole place. As you enter any room, you would hear nothing but the clasping hands and fingers of the friendly workers who were giving different kind of massage services to their clients. Kuya and Jacq went into a massage room after selecting their choice of massage.

"What made you bring me here?" Jacq asked as they were lying flat in a bed waiting for the their massage service to start.

The long blank stare from Kuya would tell Jacq he has something going on. His eyes turned red and he sounded as he had the hiccups.

"That is really a heavy cry Kuya, tell me about it," Jacq said.

"I feel a knot in my throat Jacq, this makes it so difficult for me to say what I am feeling."

"Deep breathe Kuya."

Kuya felt Jacq's caress over his bare forearm and was wet with his friend's own tears.

"Tell me so Kuya."

Kuya shared his story of what he heard of Foto, of what just had happened to him, and the conflicts he has with his family and Foto's family.

"Despite everything Jacq, I love Foto so much. She is my only definition of love."

"I understand Kuya."

"I couldn't face the world without her and thinking of losing her is an impending death."

"You have to find the truth Kuya."

"I will."

"Sir. Sir." Kuya was awaken from soft touch from one of the employees of the saloon.

"Oh my God, I overslept?" Kuya said.

He found himself soundly asleep in the room where they had their massage with Jacq earlier. He put on his top shirt on went seeking for Jacq. The receptionist explained to him that Jacq had already left.

On the way back to his car, Kuya got a voicemail: Kuya, I didn't wake you up. You went to sleep as your tears were drying up. Don't you worry; I would set an appointment for you and Foto to meet tomorrow. Take care, Jacq.

Kuya felt a throb on his chest and his lips went pale. "What I am supposed to say to Foto?" he asked.

It has been a long drive for Kuya from the saloon. So he stopped by his favorite place, the pier.

He scanned the pier as he once did in better times. The laborers on the Pier were coming up and down from a boat. He sat down before a seawall and hanged his feet over. He was watching those kids diving into the water. The cheers of those kids reminded him of Fotos' voice, smile, and laughter. "Foto has the most beautiful voice I've ever heard."

During their happy days, Kuya and Foto were always together: riding on his bike with Foto at his backseat leaning forward and kissing his neck and sing him some songs, their favorite songs ofcourse. They love to go to lakes, rivers, and mountains and took pictures everytime they have a chance. Later on, Foto would paint some of those pictures on a canvass. Simply a perfect couple, most people would love to say that. But now, Kuya is bothered with what he exactly feels and what he should think of Foto.

"She's a whore. I saw her dating with a young Korean guy. She is with her suitor when she jogs in the morning. You cannot bring in any other woman in this house."—All those are haunting Kuya's thought.

So many voices are pinching Kuya's mind but the most remarkable of all is the voice of Jacq's telling: Find out the truth, and whatever it is, you must be able to bear it all if you truly love her.

"Excuse me Sir, we're closing the Pier now," the security guard was telling him to leave.

Close to 3 in the morning when Kuya reached home. He emptied his mind as he lay down in his bed hoping to come up with better ideas in the next few hours.

"Kring. Kring." Kuya's phone rings. A text message showed on the screen which said: Kuya, after lunch at Athlatta beach resort. Kuya recited some prayers thoughtfully. He forced himself to face Foto after new develops.

Athlatta beach is one of the newest resorts in town. Its vast shore embracing the clear azure water attracts foreign visitors. It has native design cottages that were well constructed in different locations. The huge pool is located at the center but it's only exclusive to customers who would check-in for an overnight stay. Upon reaching the resort, Kuya registered himself at the reception area which he found Jacq's and Foto's name. "Where are they?" he asked as he scanned the nearby cottages. Kuya walked through the pebbled pathway heading to the main cafeteria beside the shore. It's a long walk and his eyes were entertained by the floral arrangement and the garden on every corner of the resort. His eyes were frozen when it got contact with Foto who is busy talking with Jacq. He felt ice under his feet and his steps became heavy. His heart is filled with joy in seeing Foto but his out-of-words to say. He wanted to give her a warm embrace but his mind is telling him she's a cheater.

"Kuya." Jacq shouted at him to come over. Foto run towards him to greet him with a big hug but Kuya resisted it.

"Something wrong?" Foto asked.

"Hmmmmm. Nothing. Let's take a sit."

They ordered some food and drinks and chatted for a while yet Kuya remained silent the whole time.

"I'll get something from the car guys, and take your time. I'll be right back," Jacq said.

Foto noted Kuya's silence. She looked into his eyes and noted a cold look. Kuya grabbed Foto's hands and gave her a log soft kiss. He sat next to her and kissed her continuously. "I missed you so much Foto. And I love you still."

"But tell me Foto, do you love me still?"

"Kuya? What made you asked such a thing?"

"I know, that you were dating many different men. Please, whatever you do Foto . . . . do not deny this fact!"

Foto laughed out loud which offended Kuya.

"I'm serious Foto!"

"Okay Kuya."

Foto hugged and kissed him. Kuya wanted to resist her . . . but he could not. He missed her, needed her and longer for her touch.

"Yes I dated with my student," Foto started to explain.

Kuya found out that Foto had been teaching Korean students to speak the English language. At their last session, her students would usually take her out for a dinner date as a gratitude for her being patient with them. On the other hand, that guy that Foto went with every morning during a jog session is her suitor. Foto loves to jog and she was glad to have this guy as a companion and also for safety. Lately, the guy found her interesting as most guys do, thus she stopped going with this guy because she already have Kuya. Upon knowing these, shame grew inside of Kuya but still he had more issues to point out against Foto.

"What about the black magic? The spell? How much did you pay for them to make me crazy over you?"

"What's going on with you Kuya?"

"Do you understand the challenges of living while a spell was cast upon me? The pain that I could not explain and the death wish as well that I had to live with."

Kuya talked endlessly that Foto couldn't follow him at all. He's not listening to Foto that made Foto screamed inorder for him to hear her at once.

"Kuyaaaaaaaa! If you couldn't love me, then don't love me. Just don't let your ethnic beliefs ruin your educational level. I'm a law student with a bachelor's degree and you're thinking I'm such naïve?"

Kuya went hysterical. He couldn't control his mixed emotions. And he's saying things out of his mind. Words simply burst from his mouth. Harsh words that stabbed Foto's heart.

"What about the rumor at the gym?"

"What rumor Kuya? Which gym?"

"You had several sexual affairs in your Karate club! Tell me the truth whore!!!"

The last word of Kuya ambushed Foto's heart with rage. Her tears seethed fast laced with anguish and pain. She wanted to hit Kuya hard on his face but her love for Kuya stopped her from doing so. She sobbed endlessly and heavily and just left without extra words said.

"There's no more us Kuya. No more. This is just a hopeless case. I was so hopeful at first. But now you just showed me your other side."

"What had I have done?" Kuya said.

Kuya couldn't feel his body. He saw Foto running away fast. He wanted to stop her but he couldn't move a single muscle of his body.

Jacq is approaching fast to Kuya's location.

"What's wrong Kuya?" Jacq asked. "I saw Foto ran and she's leaving us?"

"I just made the biggest mistake of my life."

They had a short discussion then both left the resort. On their way home, Kuya was trying to contact Foto at all cause but he failed. He dropped Jacq at the city then he went home.

"BEEP. BEEP."

Someone opened Kuya's gate. He parked his car. He stepped out from the car and saw her mom at the garden close to his parent's house.

"I love you mom."

Kuya kissed his mom and sat beside her.

"What's wrong Son, tell me?"

His mom could tell something just had happened.

"I just lost my battle."

"Do you want to be alone?"

"Just stay Mom."

"I think it's our fault Son."

"Mom."

"Yes. If only we didn't interfere with your love affair, you must be one of the happiest persons in this world now."

"I agree Son." His father just said who happened to hear their conversation.

"I was listening, and I heard everything so I came to talk with you."

"Dad, it's too late."

"We couldn't have everything Son. But the worse thing is to lose the one we hope to be with."

"But Son, you deserved to be happy now," his mom said.

"Yes son. You have your own house, cars, some business, and a stable job," his dad said.

"I do Dad. Yet what these things would offer me if I lose the one I love?"

"Forgive us Son. Your mom and I we've been talking for moths after our last argument and we found our fault. We were guilty of all your frustrations now."

"You are still my parents and I love you."

"Thank you Son. Whatever your plans are, we will support you," his dad said.

Despite all the sadness and failures Kuya had for the day, he still find happiness from the support his parents are now giving him.

Kuya realized how he ruined Foto's life. Foto who is a very descent woman became a victim of false accusations and has nothing to do with all the allegations against her. She knew only one thing and that is to love Kuya. Despite these, Kuya were blinded from the wrong information given by his trusted friends without giving them a second thought. He wrote an apology letter to Foto's mom. He was planning to ask forgives to Foto's family in person yet shame stopped him. In his letter, Kuya promised that he would stop communicating with Foto yet his love for her would subsist and when would it end, Kuya had no answer.

Days later, Kuya went back to work. Away from home, he tried to forget all the sad memories he had with Foto yet his love would always bring him back to those days where they shared love together. It was difficult for Kuya to move on. He tried dating with select girls yet no one has been able to replace Foto in his heart.

Almost two years had passed, yet Kuya still loved Foto. Kuya felt this was the time to get married due to his age. He searched for a wedding planner from a Facebook—an internet engine where you could find friends and post anything like a business or so. He found Nora—a skilled wedding planner who happened to be connected with Foto, a friend in fact.

"Who's the bride?" Nora asked.
"I will tell you soon," Kuya said.
"When would this be?"
"Soon."
"But you need to get a marriage license before you can get married."
"Leave it to me Nora. Trust me."
Months passed quickly. Kuya went back home to celebrate holidays with his family and friends.
He first landed in Ebuc city. He paid a surprised visit to his other ex-girlfriend, not Foto. After few days of dating with his ex, he finally went back to his own city.

He phoned his friends right away and hanged out with them in a disco bar where they usually meet. He was trying to find out from them about all his ex-girlfriends since he had a few.
"Don't tell me Kuya you're planning to select a bride from your ex-girlfriends?" a friend asked.
"I think that is the story here." Another friend said and they all laughed.
Kuya found out that one of his ex-girlfriend is getting married in a few days time. It seems Kuya is losing his chances in finding a bride this time.
"What about Nami, your parent's choice?" a friend asked.

"She is in Ebuc city now but she's coming over this holiday."

"So you're not planning to propose to her? She's pretty, fine, smart, and most of all, you're relatives like her most from the rest of your girls."

Kuya didn't answer his friend's comment; instead he ordered more foods and drinks.

"I heard Foto is having a PhD boyfriend now," a friend teasing him.

"That's great. Atleast she's happy now."

Kuya's phone beeps and a text message showed, "Kuya, your marriage license is ready." There was another voicemail from Nora. Nora left word that everything was ready for his nuptials . . . all except for the bride.

From his phone, Kuya scanned his Facebook and found lady friends—a law student, a medical student, and the list go on.

"Come on guys let's go home," Kuya inviting everyone to go home and he is in a hurry.

"But Kuya it's too early," his friends protested.

They all went out from the bar. Kuya dropped his friends in a bus station and he went looking for a potential bride. His phone beeps again. "Are the bridesmaid ready?" a message from Nora.

"Shoot! I'm missing one more bridesmaid," Kuya said.

He stopped in the city's boulevard—the most beautiful place to hang out at night in the city. The bright lights keep the by-standers awake and the street's foods are ready for everybody's belly. He ordered some fish-ball and tempura as he was thinking of his situation.

"Hi Kuya, welcome back. How are you?"

He was surprised to see one of Nami's friends. For years they don't see each other.

"I'm fine. Could I pick you up in few days' time and I'll treat you somewhere," Kuya said.

Nami's friend offered no refusal at all. Kuya was enjoying his night at the boulevard then he finally came up with a plan. For days Kuya was dating with select friends, the ones he found from Facebook. They all look great and with a descent background. "But there's no spark," Kuya said to himself. Kuya is left with no other choice but Nami. Nami was his ex-girlfriend for years and his parent's favorite. Nami lived with his parents for a while before she went to Ebuc city. And now she's coming over for the holiday.

Five days before the wedding. Kuya fetched Nami from the Pier. He then told her of his plan about the wedding. Nami showed no emotion yet she agreed. After all, she loves him that much. Kuya and Nami didn't tell anyone about the wedding even their parents have no idea of it including their closest friends. They were all busy with the preparations.

The wedding day finally came yet Kuya and Nami appeared calm and relax pretending that they know nothing about what is about to happen.

The wedding day came at last and Kuya is busy getting all people involved ready.

"Dad and Mom, I have some clothes for you," Kuya said.

Kuya gave his parents some instructions. His parents have to be in Rahuba resort before 4 pm.

"What's the affair Son?" his dad asked.

"We'll have some swimming and dinner."

"Wow, that's really great!"

Kuya picked up the entire bridesmaids who have no idea that they are going to be bridesmaid in an instant. They all thought they were all going to a resort to swim and to eat. All of them were so excited to see Rahuba resort—one of the province's most luxurious resorts. However, they were shocked when Kuya took all their mobile phones away. "Kuya why?" one of the bridesmaid was complaining. Kuya explained that he would return all their phones back upon his return. Kuya left them in a villa inside the resort.

The resort is so huge that you need a car to travel from the main entrance going down to its cottages. Giant coconut trees were all around and were swaying because of a moderate sea breeze. There's a big pool at the center of the resort with different depths. And beautiful villas and cottages were scattered beautifully all over the place.

"What a lucky day!" one of the bridesmaid said.

As the bridesmaid walked towards their assigned villa, they saw some workers from the resorts that were busy preparing for a party. A long red carpet was placed on the green grassy ground, and white tulips were scattered over the carpet. Chairs and tables were grouped accordingly and an altar was placed to where the carpet ends. At the side of the altar was a long table covered by a white mantel and a big flower bouquet on its very center. There were torches standing surrounding the garden. A separate tent was made at a corner with big sound system set inside, and a man busy tuning in his saxophone.

"Is this a wedding?" a bridesmaid asked.

"How I love to witness a wedding party," another bridesmaid said.

Before Kuya finally left the resort, he went to see Nora who was busy at the garden directing all her staffs.

"Hey Nora," Kuya greeted her.

"Kuya, where are they?"

"At the villa as you told me earlier."

"That's great! I'll send my make-up artists right now."

"Great! Great!"

Kuya left the resort to picked-up some other guests while Nora went to see the girls.

"Hi, I'm Nora," she introduced herself.

"Hello," the girls responded in unison.

"The bridesmaids that Kuya selected are gorgeous, I'm really glad!" Nora said.

"Bridesmaids???" they all scream in surprised!

Kuya came back together with some friends and select cousins—the grooms' men. He then introduced them to Nora.

"Groomsmen? We are?"

All of them gave different facial expressions upon knowing that they were going to perform some roles.

"And your emcee Kuya?" Nora asked.

"Him!" Kuya pointed at his close friend who just got home from Italy.

"Me?" "You told me it's a beach party Kuya?"

Kuya heard some laughter. The camera man and the photographers were busy filming and taking pictures.

"By the way, whose wedding is this? I have to know okay?" the emcee asked.

"It's Kuya's and . . . . and his bride I think," Nora explained.

"Kuya's???

His friends looked at him at Kuya started running away. They all run after him towards the pool, the garden, and everywhere. Kuya ran fast because his surprised friends would want to kick his behind.

"I didn't wear my underwear thinking I'm going to swim," the emcee said.

Everybody laughed out loud and shared their stories on how Kuya invited them.

"Kuya said it's a dinner."

"He told me a pool party."

"A birthday celebration."

"Mine is worse from you all, the emcee said. He told me we're going to talk about some business and I was so interested on it. So I booked right away from Italy because he told me it's going to happen so soon and if I missed it, then he would look for somebody else. I just landed yesterday and still have some jet lags. I woke up from his call this afternoon and asked me to come in 30 minutes to this resort because the resort would close eventually. I didn't realize I don't have my underwear on. Thank God I have some pants atleast. I did not take my shower. And now I'm the emcee?"

Everyone's fun was shattered upon the arrival of Kuya's parents and relatives who were all well-dressed.

"So Kuya's family knew?" somebody from the crowd asked.

Kuya's families were approaching the crowd. They looked natural but were also wondering on what is going on especially when they noticed there were several others who came.

"Are we all here for same dinner?" Kuya's dad asked.

Everybody just laughed.

Kuya's dad was amazed and surprised in knowing it was Kuya's wedding.

Nami's families were approaching from behind. They were well-dressed too for the occasion. However, it is obvious that Nami's mom was bringing along with her a gift.

"A Christmas wrap?" someone from the crowd said in a very loud voice.

Giggles and teasing and laughing were heard all over. Nami's families thought it would be for a Christmas party.

More visitors came and similar to the rest, they were not aware of anything.

"You're the bestman," Kuya said.

"Me?"

"You're one of the sponsors."

"A sponsor?"

"You're one of the witnesses. Cord. Veil."

Kuya just point his fingers to anybody and kept surprising them.

Finally, the wedding proper commence. The assigned groups and individuals marched accordingly as to how Nora arranged them. Most of them were restless because they were not dressed properly. Some were fortunate to have a perfect pair of dress from top to bottom. Unfortunately others were wrongly paired and sized, but still they have to march. One of the groomsmen had a pair of long sleeves and short pants with an oversized slipper. A mixed feeling of surprised, joy, and fun aired in the whole crowd but nobody shed a tear at all.

After a long sermon, the preacher asked: where's the marriage contract? Kuya looked surprised and asked Nami instead. Kuya had no idea where exactly that contract is. He asked someone to take some documents in a folder inside the villa. After awhile, someone handed the documents to the preacher. "This is not the one," the preacher said. "I'm sorry preacher, that's my car's registration papers," Kuya said.

Another moment of laughter strokes everyone. Fortunately the preacher had some blank copies of a marriage contract.

"Kuya, do you take Nami as your wife?" the preacher asked.

"Tot. Tot. Tot." A phone rings.

"I'm sorry preacher, I have a text message," Kuya said.

"Kuya, you're getting married," Nami said.

"Oh no, the message says, YES!"

Kuya and Nami and are now lawfully husband and wife. Picture taking took place and a memorable reception followed at the garden near the seashore. And they were all entertained by romantic love songs from a saxophone. And they all shared happiness and love.

Another reception is waiting at Kuya's house. Like the visitors in the resort, Kuya's guests at his house know nothing about the event.

The newlywed couple arrived at the house. Everyone's eyes were wondering if this is for real. They see Kuya and Nami in full white dress but they thought the couple had just attended a costume party, a birthday celebration, or a Christmas party.

"I thought they were going to visit their late grandma at the cemetery," one of the visitors said.

Some of the guests saw the wedding cake, but they still don't believe Kuya got married. "He has no girlfriend at all," someone from the crowd said.

The live band continuously playing love songs but the emcee went on stage to formally announce what had happened at the resort.

"Please join me in welcoming the newlywed couple."

Cheers and laughter collided and all the speculations ended at once.

The wedding celebration ended with lighted Chinese lanterns. They sky was filled with beautiful brilliant lanterns pushed by the wind and they looked like twinkling stars from a distance.

Everyone is now waving goodbye. Kuya was alone on the second floor of his house where they fly the lanterns earlier. Kuya was watching the lanterns closely.

"Bye Kuya," Jacq said.

Kuya wave for a response.

"Something is wrong," Jacq said. "His eyes were unhappy. I know him. I know him for sure."

The sky is bright, the wind is cool, but it was a quite night for Kuya. He secluded himself from the rest of his friends who were drinking some wine and were having some singing moment at the first floor of his house. Kuya had some heavy drink earlier that put him to sleep. Kuya slept at the terrace of the second floor. Kuya woke up the following morning later than anticipated.

"It's late Kuya. Now, talk to me," his dad said. Kuya was surprised to see his dad beside him. His dad looks so serious with burning eyes filled with emotions.

"What made you decide to marry Nami?" his dad asked.

"That's the way it should be Dad."

"Stop that nonsense!" his dad's voice reached the third floor of the house.

"Aren't you still happy and satisfied Dad? What else should I do dad to make you happy?"

"Yes, we're happy to have you choose Nami but to marry her for our sake and not because you love her—is foolishness Son! It's a big damn foolishness!"

"But Dad . . ."

"Yes my son! We prefer Nami to be your partner. But to see my son's heart bleeding for a lifetime is a curse."

"What do you want me to do Dad? I'm confused."

Do what you have to do when you still have a chance."

"But what about Nami?"

"I and your mom would take care of her."

"Thank you Dad."

Kuya hugged his dad like he was missing him for years. He hurriedly dressed himself and went to see Nora, the wedding planner.

"Beep. Beep. Beep."

Kuya was beeping at Nora's gate endlessly. The gate opened and Nora looked annoyed of the noise but after seeing Kuya, she was apologetic.

"What on earth brought you here early this morning Kuya?"

Kuya just kissed Nora and jumped for joy. He was shaking Nora's hands and didn't know exactly on what to say.

"Did you do it according to what I tell you?" Kuya asked.

"Did what?"

"I told you to process all my documents in order to get my marriage license, right?"

"Yes, and?"

"Yes! Yes! Thank you Nora. So, we'll do Plan-B."

"Plan-B? Hey what's Plan-B Kuya?"

Kuya just left without saying a word. He phoned Jacq to contact Foto and begged her to bring Foto to the place where he is heeding now. Jacq had no idea on what's going to happen. Kuya is a mysterious guy and full of plans ahead. Jacq did contact Foto and asked her to come with her.

Sunset is coming at the shore of Dyonbi's town. There is a resort in Dyonbi where Kuya loves most when Foto brought him once over. Kuya asked the owner of the resort a favor. Kuya wanted one of the cottages to be exclusive tonight and arrange it according to his plan. Meanwhile, Jacq did her best to bring Foto to the resort as instructed by Kuya. Jacq gave her best excuses, of which she is really good at, just to convince Foto to come with her. It was a 3-hour journey going to the resort.

"I'm not coming out," Foto insisted.

"But we're here. Come on let's get out from my car and we'll enjoy the sunset at the shore.

"No, I'm not going!" Foto started to raise her voice.

"Any reason?"

"This place had so many memories for me and Kuya. I couldn't handle this."

"Foto, you can't run away from your memories and fears. Just let it go and God will fight your battles for you."

Finally, the two went out from the car. They were enticed on how the place was prepared. Lighted Chinese lanterns were hanged by the main entrance towards a center cottage where more lanterns were hanged brilliantly. As they walked towards the cottage, they were serenaded with violins. Foto saw two sailboats, from where she stood, at the sea filled with lighted candles and each candle was safely placed inside a cube lantern which made it glow beautifully. As they moved closer, they noticed *Sampaguita* petals scattered over the pathway heeding to the cottage. The scent of these *Sampaguita* flowers brought some souls to their nostrils.

"I couldn't take this any further," Foto said and she was turning her back away.

"What's wrong Foto?"

"I can feel his presence. Everything that is happening now was exactly the things he told me when he is going to . . . ." Foto swallowed her last words.

"When he is going to what Foto? Say it!"

"Forget it! It's odd to think of it. I need to go back."

Foto is about to leave when she noted some writings attached to each lantern hanging on the cottage. Together, they start reading each one.

"You came not to defeat me, but to refine me."

"I left you for us to consider things, but I kept you locked in my heart."

"Fight for your love, I'm fighting for mine now."

"We need to be happy now, not in later times."

"If you leave now, make sure you carry your heart with you."

Finally, the last note was hanging over the center table which says: I left my love here; I came to get it back.

Right after they read out the last note, the serenade from the violins stopped, and the lighted lanterns turned off. They almost shout for fear when they realized a single candle is still burning from a distance.

"Jacq, don't scare me like this," Foto said and started to shiver.

"Me too Foto. That last candle is coming to us?" Jacq felt cold when she saw the candle moving towards them.

"I was lost but I found my way back here," someon is speaking out indistinctively in a loud voice.

"Kuya?" Foto shouted inside her mind.

Yes that was Kuya and he continued to speak aloud. He was pouring out his hearts to Foto. Foto looked back and she couldn't Jacq this time. "Did

Jacq run away," Foto asked in her mind. Suddenly, Kuya is now infront of her holding the last candle infront of them.

"This is the very last candle left lighted in this resort. And I'm protecting it from the wind to guide my way here. If you will, are you going to blow the light out?"

Foto did not understand what Kuya was trying to drive at. Kuya looked her straight and asked her again.

"I can't Kuya. I can't."

"Why?"

"If I do that, we can't find our way back, and I'm scared."

"Foto hugged Kuya tight. She's shivering. Kuya made her comfortable with his embrace.

"Calm down, I'm here—so is my love for you. I was scared too and made many mistakes. This is my last chance to have you back."

Foto felt surging ache from her belly. She was joyful to feel once again the embrace of Kuya yet the pains from Kuya's harsh words two years ago still linger in some portion of her heart. Yet her overwhelming love convinced her that she must trust his words this time.

"You despised me Kuya and you believed on that stupid rumor about me. And you get married to Nami?"

"I never hate you. How could you love a person and hate the person back? I never believed on that rumor, not a single story of it."

"But what about the marriage?"

"In the eyes of the people, I'm a married man. But under our constitution, I'm not."

Kuya explained that he fixed the marriage with the helped from Nora. He used a decoy to get a marriage license for him. And his signature was forged too. And they were signing black documents.

"How could I get a marriage license when I was in another city during the time my documents were being processed?"

Kuya showed Foto some legal documents from his lawyer explaining that his case was a *Void Ab intio* which means, no marriage ever happened between him and Nami.

Kuya saw some tears glared from Foto's brown eyes when Foto realized Kuya didn't fail their love for each other. A moment of joy and love made them one again. Kuya held Foto's hands and they went to the shore where two sailboats await them. The violins serenade them as they crossed the shoreline. Kuya picked up Foto from her waist line and positioned her inside the sailboat. A bottle of wine and two empty Riedel's glass wine were set-up on a table. They sat side-by-side together.

"This is like a fantasy Kuya," Foto said.

"Remember what I told you when we were at your aunt's rest house?"

"Hmmmm . . . Oh my God, Kuya?"

"Yes."

Kuya took a small heart-shaped red box under the table. He took Foto's left hand and kissed her fingers. Foto's heart raced with thrills and joy. She felt her heartbeats over her chest.

"Foto, will you marry me?"

Foto couldn't find a word to response. Her glance was focused at the ring Kuya is now holding at the very instant.

"Say YES!"

There were some commotions from the other sailboat. Nora and Jacq were teasing them. There were two other guys too onboard where Nora and Jacq were, and these guys have a flute and a violin with them. All of them were hiding inside that sailboat and just came out as instructed by Kuya previously.

"We couldn't afford another make-believe marriage Foto," Nora shouted against the blowing wind.

"Or an annulment maybe?" Jacq said with a laugh.

Foto remained speechless while the rest of her buddies were happily teasing them.

"Yes. Yes. Yes. Say Yes now Foto."

Kuya touched Fotos' lips and said, "Would my kiss be able to bring out the words from your heart?"

"Just kiss me Kuya. And kiss me more."

"Yahoo!" Jacq cheered them.

"Should I begin a wedding plan?" Nora asked.

They began sailing back to the city. The serenade was continuously playing as Kuya and Foto were sharing their love back to each other. A wedding was set and they were all excited for the upcoming wedding.

This is the love story of Kuya and Foto—the love Kuya and Foto has has been tested and proven over the course of time. The love that these two souls have extend beyond human's ability to comprehend. The love they share does not give up. Instead this love endures forever. A love that simply wants to be owned to where it should belong.

Heartbroken

"Get out of my room immediately!"

Mr. Paul, a male patient in a nursing home, with an early diagnosis of Dementia shouted at his wife. Mr. Paul's Dementia made him forget a lot of things. This included his wife whom he used to love very much. Despite the fact that he ignored his wife, she continued to visit him to provide care. Then one unfortunate day his wife was diagnosed with brain cancer and could no longer take care of Mr. Paul.

"Leticia, Leticia. Hello Leticia. Leticia . . . hello."

Leticia, the young daughter of Mr. Paul, was unable to recognize the call from Ray, her boyfriend. Leticia was deep in thought while she watched her mom lying helpless in the recovery room of Flushing Hospital in New York. She was deeply moved by her emotions making her less aware of what was going on around her until a gentle touch from Ray one her shoulder disturbed her.

"I'm so sorry Ray," Leticia said.
"I understand. Are you crying again?" Ray asked.
"I can't help it Ray, all of this is so sudden," Leticia said.
"How's your mom doing?" Ray asked.
"There's less and less signs of life. It's so disheartening! She used to be jovial and funny and loving to all of us especially Dad but look at her now."
"She's a shell of the woman we loved and knew," Leticia said.

Her head on Ray's shoulder, Leticia began to reminisce about her mom.

Leticia's mom was involved in all the aspect of her life, homework, to how to choose a good husband. Even though her mom was busy at work, she still found time to care for Dad in the nursing home and always made time for me.

Leticia knew how much her parents loved one another by the beautiful stories she was told until one afternoon her mom came home crying. Her mom tried to reassure her that everything was fine, but Leticia knew better.

"What's wrong Mom? Your dress is soaking wet," Leticia said.
"Your Dad," her mom replied in short sobbing breaths.
"What did Daddy do to you Mom? Please tell me," Leticia asked wiping the tears that flowed down her Mom's cheeks.

Leticia tried to make her mother as comfortable as possible by bringing her fresh clothing and a cup of brisk, hot tea. Finally her mom began to tell her what happened earlier that afternoon. Hours before, her mom visited her dad in the nursing home. She had entered his room and greed him with a kiss as she usually did each time she visited. Her mom expected the kiss to be reciprocated, but to her mom's surprise, her dad began to yell and demanded she leave his room at once. At first, her mom paid no attention because she was aware of her husband's dementia problem. She attempted to comfort him by giving him some more food to eat along with hot brewed coffee which was his favorite. As time went on he became agitated for no good reason, and threw the cup of coffee on her mom's face. She screamed in pain as the coffee burned her face and neck. Hearing the commotion, the nurse came running in the room. The nurse provided first aid to mom and calmed dad down with a tranquilizer. Leticia realized this was by far, the worst her father ever treated her mother. She was aware on previous visits he had cursed and swore and even tried to hit her mom, but it was never this bad. Though Leticia realized these reactions were a result of her father's mental state, it horrified and saddened her. She wondered how her mom could continue to love him, and return everyday to care for him. He was now so different from the man he used to be. Leticia marveled even more when though being severely ill herself, she continued to struggle to maintain her vigil by her husband's bedside. Eventually, her mom's illness took its toll and she herself required hospitalization.

"I'm so sorry to hear all this," Ray said, trying to interrupt her as he kissed her on her cheek.

"Are you leaving?" Leticia asked.

"Hmm . . . not really but I'm trying to focus on my job right now," Ray said.

"Would you mind spending few more hours with me? I feel so sad and down," Leticia said.

Leticia tried to convince Ray to stay, but Ray though sympathetic, insisted on leaving. Leticia understood that Ray was busy with his job, but the fact he'd be relocating soon, made Leticia even more worried.

Leticia watched Ray unloading the bag filled with groceries and beverage from the car. Leticia felt comforted by seeing the one she loved being so helpful. Ray's presence had the ability to calm her. His encouraging manner lifted her mood and his caresses and kisses comforted her. In short she simply couldn't imagine life without him.

Ray seemed suddenly quiet and withdrawn. Leticia came from behind him, hugged him and said, "A penny for your thoughts, Ray." He blurted all at once, I've been meaning to tell you, "Leticia, I have a baby," Ray said.

Leticia stared at him in disbelief—who was this stranger standing before her?

"Whatttttttttttttttttttttt?" Leticia yelled.

For a moment she forgot she was in a recovery with her mom.

"I was just kidding. YOU ARE MY BABY," Ray calmly said.

That's not even funny, especially with all I'm going through. Whatever possessed you to say such a thing! There are some things you don't joke about.

Leticia always knew Ray had a weird sense of humor, and that he loved to tease her, but even for him this was way out there.

"But there is something I really want you to know Leticia, but this is not the proper time," Ray said, as he turned his back and looked aimlessly out of the window.

"What's that supposed to mean?" Leticia wondered. An uneasy feeling arose in the pit of her stomach, as a sense of foreboding enveloped her.

That last statement of Ray's bothered Leticia very much. She recalled to mind how Ray used to tell her that he wanted to straighten out things in his life. She wanted to talk with Ray, but she knew Ray didn't have enough time right this minute, besides her main concern was her mom. Ray left while she kept her vigil with her mom.

Month's passed and though Leticia's mom tried to recover her body was not cooperating. Leticia saw the determination of her mom to survive, yet the proof of her eyes and the doctor's reports, held slim hope for recovery. Leticia tried to put on a brave face for her mom's sake, but accepted the possibility that she might lose her mom at any moment. Even in her mom's weakened state, her mom continued to advise her in so many ways. She also told her how happy she was to have had her dad who love her so deeply all her life. Her mom's love story always brought inspiration to Leticia. Day by day her mom's voice grew weaker, she did not fail to say "I love you" to Leticia and her dad. "I ALWAYS SAY I LOVE YOU NOT BECAUSE I LOVE TO REPEAT IT, BUT BECAUSE IT IS THE MOST TRUTHFUL FEELING I KNOW, AND I DON'T KNOW HOW TO SAY IT BETTER," her mom said. Her mom's words not only encouraged her to stay strong in life, but also made her realize how beautiful it is to love someone and have that love returned completely.

"I miss you so much Ray. I just want to hold you and be in your arms," Leticia said to herself. It was awhile now since Ray called her. She was wondered at Ray's long silence. Time was when Ray used call and leave a message. Or he'd email or chat with her on the web. Now though so much time had passed she didn't even know where he was. Why is he withdrawn and silent she thought? Leticia longed to know what was going on with Ray, but her mom deserved her undivided attention. Thoughts of Ray would have to be put on hold for now.

Leticia saw her mom squealing in excruciating pain. She couldn't walk because every move would precipitate gnawing pain. She wanted to help but no amount of analgesic could relieve the soreness. It struck the bones. She saw her mom lose her shiny, black, beautiful hair, and her nails. Leticia saw her mom's insomnia because her source of breathing was compromised. Her mom had only one feeble lung struggling for survival. Leticia saw her mom losing ground daily. She was in constant pain. The light diminishes from her mom's eyes. Her liver was compromised. It was clear her mom would never leave this death-bed.

Leticia saw her mom move and was trying to speak but nothing was audible. Leticia found out her mom had recently lost her voice completely due to radiation treatments and chemotherapy. Leticia offered her mom a pen and a paper on which to write, but her mom was too weak to hold the pen. Leticia felt unbelievably saddened both by her mom's increasingly weakened state, but even more by not having the words of wisdom her mom still wanted to impart. Leticia moved the bedside table closer to her mom to make it easier to reach. She told her mom that she'd be back early the next day straight from her job. Leticia left the room and called the nurse to tell her she was leaving and make sure her mother was adequately cared for.

The next day, Leticia was not able to see her mom before she went to her regular radiation treatment but her mom left her a note on the table. It was very hard for Leticia to decipher what her mom was trying to tell her through her distorted handwriting. The note read, "Dearest Leticia, please visit your dad for me and take good care of him. If he is able to understand, ask him how he loves me and bring his message back to me. Leticia's heart was filled with excitement, because she wanted to know more details of her parent's love story. She left the hospital at once, and went to her dad in the nursing home.

As Leticia took the train, she wished Ray was beside her. She loved how he talked to her and shared jokes, teased, and made her laugh. All of a sudden, her phone rang. It was Ray. Leticia's excitement made her heart leap to see Ray's name on the caller ID. Just as she was about to answer Ray, the signal was lost as the train entered a tunnel. The moment the train surfaced, she grabbed her phone and tried to catch Ray, but he was already gone. Suddenly she got a voice mail from Ray telling her to be online in an hour so that they can chat on the web. Leticia decided to drop-by Main Street, Flushing where an internet café was accessible. With bated breath she waited for Ray to come online at the appointed time.

Leticia ordered some caramel coffee to calm her nerves as she waited patiently for Ray to connect. She finished her two cups of coffee and apple pie yet there was no sign of Ray. When the clock struck 7, she realized she had to leave to visit her dad at the nursing home. She was clear about the rules that visiting hours were only to 9 pm. Leticia was extremely frustrated with the situation between her and Ray. She left Ray an offline message: "*I am tired of the pretense. I am tired of being on again and off again with you with no explanation. I want to get straight to the point, in simple and plain language. I am totally frustrated by the distance, the flaws and the complexities of our relationship. I want to know once and for all what I mean to you and if you consider what we've had a relationship or not. Ray I cannot take any more pain.*

You made me wait for an hour, and then didn't call. I just want to get a decent, truthful discussion about what is going on. I do not want to beg, nor will I, for one precious moment of your time. I am a person with dignity and deserve better treatment. Consider my feelings enough to keep the appointment. I know you're there. Your silence was very discouraging. It drained all my strength and made me weak. I am weak and I am giving up. I guess I need space. I want to take one pain at a time. I guess I have to contemplate and reflect on my mother's condition. At this most difficult time in my life you were the only bit of comfort and happiness I had. But you see . . . . The person I've looked up to is the one who is giving me more pain than I can bear right now.

Leticia had no idea if Ray would get her offline message but she sent it anyway. She left the internet café and took a bus and went to Flushing Manor Nursing Home, which was a few minutes away from where she was now. Her mind was really troubled and now she had to face her dad, who may not be able to recognize her at all. The bus stopped in front of the nursing home's main entrance. She stepped down from the bus. She saw a few residents of the nursing home sitting outside the building and were smoking. Others simply sat alone in their wheelchairs enjoying the warm weather. She went to the information desk, and the in-charge told her that her dad was on the 6th floor. She headed to the elevator. It was a long wait in line just to get a few seconds ride. There were two elevators busily coming up and down. Finally, Leticia got a chance to take one of the elevators.

The elevator was loaded with medical staff and residents. Many of them were engaged in conversation.

"Nurse Brown, is it true that we're going to have a wedding party in the building soon?" one of the residents asked?

"Yes. Yes. Yes. We're processing it," Nurse Brown gave a hurried response.

"It will be so exciting to have a wedding here," another resident said.

"Yeah, yeah. Never mind, after the wedding the newlywed couple will call for the aides for a change of their diapers," another resident commented.

Hearing their conversations made Leticia laugh.

"It's the 6th floor," the elevator operator announced.

Leticia stepped out of the elevator and she saw how busy the floor was. The house keeper was busy mapping the floor, and a WET FLOOR sign was placed in some corners. The aroma of PINE SOL wafted up to Leticia's nose and made her sneeze. She heared call bells ringing endlessly, but it seemed no one was answering them. There were some residents playing BINGO in the DAY ROOM, while other residents are wandering the halls. Leticia went to the nurse's station to ask where her dad was.

"Could I see my father, Mr. Paul?" she asked.

"Sure ma'am, in the Day room please."

Leticia went to the Day room and searched for her dad. She scanned the room and saw her dad in a corner in a wheelchair next to few other residents. She looked at her dad with full pity. Tears started to run from her eyes. She wanted to hug her dad so badly but she was fearful that her dad might slap her just like he did to her mom. Leticia does not want to interrupt Mr. Paul from playing BINGO, but the visiting hour was nearly over. She moved slowly and approached Mr. Paul in a calm manner.

"Hello dad, it's me Leticia," she said.

"Dad? Leticia?" Mr. Paul replied.

"Yes! Your daughter," she said.

"I think you got the wrong person young girl," Mr. Paul said.

Leticia felt sad at the way her dad answered her, but she knew her dad had Dementia. Leticia requested the aide to bring her dad to his room after playing Bingo. She sat next to her dad and watched him happily playing Bingo. After the last number was called and somebody was announced as the winner, her dad himself asked the aide to go to his room. Her dad seemed upset because he didn't win the game. She followed her dad to his room.

As Leticia followed her dad at a distance, she can hear her father talking loudly to the aide. She became more scared because her dad's tone was very aggravated and she thought he might be violent later when she talked to him. The aide left the room and Leticia entered. It was a private room with ample space and a television. Leticia asked her dad if he wanted the t.v. on, or to have something to drink as they talked. Her dad refused everything. Leticia then started a conversation with her dad by asking him if he missed his wife. Unfortunately, her dad couldn't remember anybody not even the name of his wife. Then he even denied that he was ever married.

"Dad, it's me Leticia, your daughter, don't you remember? Leticia asked.
"What? A daughter? How could it be? I was never married but I'm going to be!" Her dad said.

Leticia was bothered that her dad just said, "getting married soon." "How could this be?" she asked herself. Leticia tried her best to remind her dad of her mom, but her dad got annoyed and was agitated by her repeated questions.
Leticia knew she couldn't continue the conversation. She could see her dad clinching his fists, then he began to yell and demanded she leave the room. She couldn't help but cry. She left the room and went to see the nurse who was busy doing her paper work at the station right now.

"Excuse me nurse, can you tell me more about my dad?" she asked.
"Hello Ms., I'm nurse Brown and you are?" nurse Brown said.
"I'm Leticia, Mr. Paul's daughter," she said.

Nurse Brown checked her dad's chart then told her some details about Mr. Paul. Leticia couldn't believe of what she learned from Nurse Brown. According to Nurse Brown, her dad's Dementia was getting worse. He seemed to be forgetting more and more. He even forgot his own name and he couldn't recall anybody's name at all. Eventually, her dad tried to compensate by making up stories that he has a very lovely girlfriend which was not true. As a result, her dad had to look for someone as his girlfriend to support his story. Fortunately, her dad met another confused woman in the unit who thought of Mr. Paul as her late husband. So at this time, her dad, Mr. Paul, and this other woman were engaged.

"Engaged? Did I hear you right Nurse Brown?" Leticia asked.

"Yes Ms. Leticia. I'm sorry to inform you, but we allow our residents to have a formal relationship," Nurse Brown said.

"But that's not possible because my dad is a married man," Leticia said.

"There's nothing more we can do to help our residents to be happy. Besides, this is an issue of maintaining the quality of life. Otherwise, Mr. Paul would continue his violent outburst and might hurt other residents," Nurse Brown explained.

Leticia is not happy hearing what Nurse Brown just said to her and her dad will have this so called marriage soon. Leticia took a last look at her dad before her lefr. On her way back to her dad's room, she overheard her dad talking to someone. She peeked in the door and saw her dad speaking with a woman. Leticia felt the ache in her heart travel to her stomach. She saw how happy her dad was with the other woman. He was teasing her, very cheerful and playful, just as her dad usually did with her mom. Leticia turned her back and was about to leave when her dad noticed her. "Hey young lady, come here," her dad invited. Leticia felt some joy upon her dad's request.

"Yes Mr. Paul," Leticia replied.

"I want you to meet my future beautiful wife," Mr. Paul said.

Leticia felt terrible but was trying to stay calm in front of her dad.

"Young lady, this is *Margaret*, my wife to be," Mr. Paul said.

Instead of feeling bad about what Mr. Paul said, Leticia felt a song of joy fill her heart.

"How do you address your future wife Mr. Paul?" Leticia asked with a wide smile on her face.

"*My sweet love, my only love*," Mr. Paul said.

After the short introduction by Mr. Paul, Leticia left him and his sweet love—the future wife to be. Leticia is amazed of what had happened. The tears she shed were replaced by endless smiles on her face. "*My dad really loves only one woman in his life, Ms. Margaret, the sweet love, the only love of Mr. Paul*," she said to herself.

Leticia couldn't wait a day to tell her mom about what she had found out from her dad. She took the Q13 bus back to Main Street and headed home. While in the bus, she scanned her phone, still there was no missed call from Ray, not even a voicemail message. Leticia doesn't want her happiness be mixed with her ill feelings toward Ray. She tried to put him out of her mind for as long as she could.

After an hour of travel, she is finally arrived. home. It was a long ride from the subway train and she almost fell asleep in the train. She passed by a Deli store and ordered a tuna sandwich for her dinner. She was paying at the counter when the vendor asked her about Ray. "Where's your boyfriend Ms. Leticia," the vendor asked. She offered him a smile but declined to answer. The Deli store was the place where Ray usually waited for her. The Deli store was across the street from the subway station where Leticia got off from work. Leticia and Ray usually ordered some food together from the Deli before they walked to her house. So the neighbors and by-standers go to knew them well. Leticia felt the loneliness in her heart as she walked home alone. Usually at this hour she would be waling hand in hand with Ray. Just two lovebirds all the neighborhood enjoyed seeing and admired. The more Leticia tried to forget Ray, the more he seemed to intrude her mind. She opened her main door and thought of how Ray used to block the door before opening it just to lean down and give her a kiss. Everything in her house is torturing her slowly. The pictures of Ray around the wall, the notes of "I love you" from Ray by the fridge, their pictures together in her computer monitor. Even the Tasmanian-devil-pillow that she lays on every night—reminds her of Ray. Memories keep flooding in, but she somehow managed to repress them. The next day, she prepared herself to visit her mom.

Leticia went to see her mom in Flushing hospital. She went straight to her mother's room but to her surprised she found another patient in the room. Racing pulses surged her chest as she wondered on what had happened when she was not there. She ran frantically to the nurse's station. Her excitement to see her mom was tinged with incredible sadness hearing that her mom was fighting for her life in ICU. Leticia sprints toward the ICU.

Leticia heard some commotion in the direction of the ICU as she ran. As she approached she saw nurses and doctors running back and forth into the ICU. Cold sweat formed on her forehead. She tried to get information but to no avail. Everyone was simply busy to reply. She almost fainted to see a red light flashing over the ICU room. As she reached the doo she saw how the doctors and nurses were trying to revive her mom. She was crying copious tears that were like glazed ice striking the tinted glass as she tried to catch her breath. Moments later, a man in full blue scrub suit approached her and said, "Hi, are you the daughter of Ms. Margaret?"

"Yes Sir," she replied.

"I'm doctor Scorp. I'm the doctor in-charge of your mom," the man said.

"How's my mom doc?" she asked.

"She had another attack, a severe one. Fortunately, we were able to revive her but it may not be for long," Mr. Scorp said.

When Leticia found out that her mom might not have a long life to live, she asked permission to stay with her mom in the ICU. Gratefully she entered the room and gently kissed her cheek.

Her heart was heavy, seeing her mom with all the tubes and wires connected to her body from several machines. The noise from the machines gave a panicky feeling to Leticia knowing that any change in their operation could mean death for her mom. Her mom's pale body reminded her how delicate a life is. She moved closer to her mom and with each step thinking of how her mom taught her to walk when she was little. She whispered to her mom's ear, "Mom, Leticia is here." Then she held her mom's hand and noticed how cold they were. She touched her mom's face then realized tears were flowing from her Mom's eyes. Leticia is filled with deep emotion but she wants to be brave for her mom. "Mom, I went to see Dad yesterday," she said. "You know mom what I found out? *My dad has only one sweet love in his life and he mentioned it to me—it is You—his dear Ms. Margaret,*" Leticia cheerfully said. After saying these words, she saw her mom smile, very sweetly, and then she heard a long straight beep from a machine. Then the medical team came rushing in to attend to her mom. Leticia was asked to move out of the room. She waited patiently outside the ICU then Dr. Scorp came to speak to her.

"We're very sorry. We can't help your mom this time," Dr. Scorp said.

Leticia ran hurriedly to see her mom. She hugs her tightly as she could and screams her name. There are no more words to say. She had said everything to her mom before she died that really counted. The medical team gave Mother and daughter a few moments alone, then came to take the body of Ms. Margaret.

It was a long painful day for Leticia. Memories flooded her mind of all the suffering her Mom endured with the various treatments and now she was gone. Leticia could only find comfort in making her Mom smile one last time. "Mom just waited me to find how dad loves her so—she waited so long and now she will rest in peace," Leticia said to herself.

Leticia signed some paper work in the hospital then wearily she headed home. She went straight to her bed and tried to get some sleep when she heard a beep from her home phone suggesting a voice mail. "Oh, it's Karen," Leticia said. She listens to the voicemail which says, "Hi Leticia this is Karen. Guess what, I emailed Ray recently and we chatted and he told me how much he loves you. He even told me that no matter what happens, he just wants to be with you at the end. He wishes that you could be together forever. Goodbye."

Leticia ignored the message. She thinks to herself it must be a game, another lie from Ray. She is resting in bed when her cell phone beeps and a message from Ray reads: *How are you my dear? Give me a hug before you go to bed please. Can I see you tomorrow at 3pm by the Hoffman Park across Queens' mall? See you. Bye, Ray.*

Leticia doesn't know whether to reply or not. To see him or not is mind-boggling for her. She has been through a lot these days and now Ray just popped up from nowhere right after her mother's death. She said some prayers and went to bed. The next morning, she woke up feeling so light. Perhaps all her burdens just left her after finding out her dad loved her mom so much and her Mom died know that. She thought this could be a sign to end everything, so she decided to see Ray at the park.

She intentionally went to the park ahead of time. She bought some food and beverages and read some novels as she waited for Ray. "Who knows if he will show up or not, after all he is a liar," she said to herself. The park is so beautiful filled with the purple leaves of the trees and the daffodils are scattered like sunshine under the shady trees. The ambience produced a relaxed mood though it was chilly. There were some folks practicing Tai Chi, and some young guys doing Wing Chun style of martial arts at the middle of the park. She sits by the bench at the side of the park and tried to think of nothing in particular.

"Hello ma'am," a kid startled her.

Leticia almost fell from the bench. "Jesus Christ, don't do that. You scared me," She said to the boy.

"Surprised?" Ray said.

Leticia did not notice Ray come up beside her.

"Go and play basketball with your friends," Ray said to the boy.

"Who's that boy?" Leticia asked.

"My son," Ray said.

Leticia paused for awhile. She looked around the park trying to control her emotions.

"This time is for real right?" Leticia asked.

"Yes," Ray said. "I was trying to tell you before but you wouldn't give me a chance and I didn't want you to feel bad during those difficult times," Ray added.

"So you know about my mother's loss?" Leticia asked.

"I went to the hospital yesterday and I found out," Ray said. "I'm sorry."

At this time, Ray told Leticia about his past. Leticia found out that before Ray met her, Ray had a one-night affair with a woman and this woman got pregnant. He doesn't love the woman but he was forced to get married since the woman was a lawyer and her father, is a judge so there was no option. Ray is a poor man working as a tender in Starbuck's. He had no choice and he doesn't want to go to jail. He got married to the woman, now his wife, who sent him to school in return. Ray finished his bachelor's degree through the help of his wife then he met Leticia in school where they studied together for their master's degree. Ray said, "I gave my whole heart to you the first time I saw you."

"Oh it's a lie," Leticia said.

"You may no longer believe the words I will say and have said, but they are the most truthful ones." Ray said.

Leticia continued to listen to what Ray was confiding now to her. Ray said that she was the only one who made him happy, and that the best days of his life was those he had with her. He knew he found love with Leticia, but he cannot change the fact that he is a married person and has a son. There was also the issue of responsibility for his wife as a husband and as a father. Ray's relationship with Leticia got so intense that her worried that some day he might be tempted to leave his family for her. He tried to tell Leticia about it, but doing so would mean losing her which he could not bear.

"That's enough Ray," Leticia interrupted him.

"I wanted to tell you what you mean to me, of how much I love you, of how much I wanted you to be with me forever," Ray said.

"Enough. The more you tell me, the more you are hurting me. To know that you truly love me is enough for me to carry," Leticia said.

Leticia turns her head away from Ray then she starts telling him of her feelings about what he has just said.

"You know, I don't give up easily but this is too much to handle. I need time for myself to grow and be ok, and get healed. You know I love you so much, and I waited but I lost courage . . . . I guess the most difficult thing to do about all that I've been through is to pretend that I'm ok when I am not. I cannot continue to pretend I'm a tower of strength when I'm not. I wish I had some choice about what happened to me, but it's not my choice to make, it's a burden to take."

"I really love you, Ray," Leticia said.

"I love you too," Ray said.

"I don't believe in love anymore. I thought I'd get better, but I got bitter. I don't believe in magic anymore, I want to tell you that I do not regret having loved you. Even for a short time, I was able to love you in a different way. I thank God for the patience generated along our relationship, but I realized that I am limited," Leticia said and started to cry.

Ray looked at her with sadness and he wanted to give her a kiss and a hug but didn't dare suddenly the phone rang.

"Hello," Leticia said.

"This is Nurse Brown. Are you Ms. Leticia?" Nurse Brown asked over the phone.

"Yes, go ahead," Leticia said.

"Oh hi Leticia, please don't forget at 6pm you are invited to witness your dad's wedding here at the nursing home," Nurse Brown said.

Leticia only at this moment realized that today is her dad's wedding day, and she promised him that she would attend. Leticia gave one final look at Ray, told him how much she loved him, then she left him at the park. Ray called her and pleaded for her to return. She turned and said "it's time to face reality and it's time to start a new life—a life without each other."

Because the wedding time was fast approaching, Leticia called a taxi.

In no time at all she arrived at the nursing home, but she realized she was running a little late. She moved quickly to the entrance.

As she got to the lobby of the nursing home she saw how crowded it was. The wedding ceremony started 20 minutes ago, so she missed some parts of the program. Leticia saw her dad once again in his favorite suite. Though seated in a wheelchair still he looks so handsome. The lobby is well-prepared. The choir members were in long robes. A piano played melodiously from the corner. The priest was giving his sermon to the bride and the groom although she couldn't hear the message well from her location. All the residents were properly attired in their Sunday best for the occasion. Slowly Leticia moved closer to the front to get a better look. She was surprised when she got to the front; the priest announced that the groom could now kiss the bride. Clapping of hands filled the whole lobby are. Then her dad grabbed a microphone to say something. "Thank you all for coming to my first wedding. I'm so happy to marry the love of my life, Ms. Margaret," he said.

There is a moment of laughter because they all know the bride is not Margaret. Then one mischievous resident asked her dad, "If you are going to have a baby, what would be the name?"

"If it is a boy, I will name him after me, but if it will be a girl, which we are hoping for then I will name her Leticia, because Leticia in Latin means "joy"," her dad said.

What Leticia's dad had said made Leticia very happy. So happy in fact tears of joy ran down her face. "Did you hear that Mom?" she whispered.

The whole assembly went to handshake Mr. Paul and his bride. Leticia walked through the center aisle and knelt in front of her dad and said, "Congratulations, Mr. Paul. I'm so happy for you for your wife, Margaret. I'm sure you will have a baby girl soon and you will name her Leticia. Mr. Paul, my fondest wish is for me to find a man who will love me like you love Ms. Margaret and Leticia."

The celebration continued several hours after which Leticia went home. She realized that a happy and beautiful life was prepared for her by God. She knows without a doubt that many blessings are in store for her in the future. All she has to do is be patient.